CHIP CHIP

BY

RUSTY JAQUAYS

Printing History
First Printing March 2015

ISBN:1508545375
ISBN-13: 978-1508545378

DEDICATION

I am dedicating this book to my
wife, my life, Sherri.

And also my favorite oldest
daughter, Anna.

And my favorite youngest
daughter, Lauren.

My sweet little family, my best
success.

PRELUDE

The fierce eye of a seagull locked onto the small, yellow Chip Chip who flew solo, and far from her element.

The Chip Chip surfed the wind, just inches above the whitecaps, their teeth grasping at the air, hoping to snatch her into the swallowing sea.

Without a pause, the gull banked and folded into a dive after what he believed was a quick, easy meal.

With her keen awareness the Chip Chip jogged her course an inch.

The hunter missiled into the ocean, missing his prey. The dive created a tunnel of air and atomized water. When he surfaced, he resumed the posture of a duck, bobbing in and out of sight among the waves.

From a safe distance the Chip Chip saw her attacker hoist himself back into the air. Her fear quickly healed when the dangerous gull chose to rejoin the hoard of albatross and pelicans that swarm at the stern of a Cuban fishing boat.

The frenzy of angry, hungry sea birds robbed the seemingly lost little bird of any chance to rest and find sustenance on this boat. So the Chip Chip turned off shore.

She scanned the vastness of the deep blue water and the light blue sky for any hint of another lonely boat. Perhaps the distant glint of window glass in the sun, or the faint smell of exhaust in the wind would deliver a new bearing for her to take.

Ocean-going people from many cultures welcomed the rare visit from a wild canary. Commonly named Chip Chip, they provided a small but important connection to land for the home sick sailor. Many believed them to be a good luck charm that would keep them safe so far out to sea.

For the Chip Chip a boat became its only connection to land. It would be a safe perch, offering the crumbs of meals and many insects, a respite from flying for days and nights into the wind. But most important was the condensation of sweet water that appeared at dawn on the boat's surface which provides another day of life.

On the return home and nearing landfall, the Chip Chip would erupt from her comfort zone. Beyond any human understanding, she would leave the land behind, and fly back into her mystery that waits at sea.

Perhaps her cousins who live in cages had forgotten the power of freedom. Pure instinct drove the tiny brace of feathers into the greatest unknown on the planet. Immense courage for such a small creature helped her survive the almost impossible quest to find a better home.

CHAPTER 1
YOUNG MARIO

"Oje' Poppy! Poppy, wake up! Wake your old ass up!" Young Mario's words were followed by a falsetto chuckle, and a few bird whistles.

With a great white smile and festive eyes, he tossed another handful of fish guts high into the air. Taunting the gang of sea birds into an aerial dog fight was great entertainment on the long, stream home. Feathers flew as the birds violently competed for the precious glob of protein.

Turning dangerous work into a game, as only a fisherman's son could, Young Mario's chestnut hands moved the sharp blade quickly and smoothly through last night's catch of snapper and grouper. His rhythm broke only for a second, to adjust the suspender strap across his shirtless back. It held up the clumsy yellow oilers that kept him somewhat dry and not too filthy. He also wore the white, rubber boots that were a common fashion for commercial fisherman, especially in southern waters.

Feeling a little wild today more than usual, he was determined to annoy his father who was barely awake and steering the boat with his bare feet.

Young Mario shouted, "Oje' Poppy, why is this damn old boat so slow? I've seen the American boats. They are fast, oh so fast!" Then he shook his head and looked down to his work.

He flipped another handful of guts. This time he skillfully put the wad up and over the cabin. It splattered on the bow. Following the food, the sea birds moved from the stern to the front of the boat. They clashed, and crapped all over the windshield.

Mario Senior had a five-day beard and wears an ancient, worn-to-the-shine pair of trousers, ragged and cut off just below the knees. He lifted the brim of his favorite Panama hat and pulled the soggy end of a cigar out from under his mustache. He was careful not to lose that one comfortable position on the plywood seat. It took him miles to find it.

He bellowed a phrase his son had heard many times before. "We leave home, slow, and heavy in the water. We return home slow, and heavy in the water."

Young Mario silently mimicked his father's words.

In a boss man voice, Mario Senior said, "Quit playing with those damn birds. They shit all over my boat. When you finish packing the fish, you can come clean my window. I can't see where I'm going!"

Young Mario struggled to speak through his laughter. "Don't worry about it. You can't see where you're going anyway. Yes, yes, but I'm sure that, one of these days, you might get us home."

His Father issued no response, kept his head forward. Then he raised up his flexed arm, and pumped his fist a few times, as if to say *Watch out.*

The boat showed decades of unpainted repairs and blew black smoke from the stack alongside the cabin. Indeed this boat left its port slow and heavy in the water, burdened with the weight of fuel, ice and bait. The next to impossible goal of any small boat fishermen was to replace that weight with its equal in seafood.

Young Mario plunged his thumb and forefinger into the eyes of a stiff and slimy Nassau grouper. He pulled the heavy fish from the iced sea water and saw a willing dance partner. He broke into a ridiculous moment of Salsa, but his father remained unimpressed, aloof to his Son's attempts for attention while struggling to hold back his laughter.

Young Mario was completely full of himself.

Not only was it the final leg of a long and demanding journey. But on this day, he had reached the magical age of seventeen.

He had said nothing of it during the whole trip and waited to see if his father remembered his birthday. Mario Senior was well aware of the special day, but he never mentioned it. He acted as though it was no different than any other day.

Cℜ℞

After the catch is weighed in, the dock master, Warappo, allows them to keep a few of the unmarketable fish. Only on occasion would he ever show any generosity in his domain of the fish house.

Warappo was a grumpy, sweaty old man who always reeked of rum. His open shirt was stained with the day's consumption. It shows the bluish outline of his liver, welted up on his swollen stomach.

Young Mario was always repelled by this man, and gave him a wide berth. He knew the big rusted blade in Waroppo's belt had a long history of violence.

The father was overly jovial, as was his effort to crack the dark demeanor of the knife-scarred dock master.

When Mario Senior signed the government receipt and they untied their boat from the fish house, the father and son idled across the postcard harbor of Los Villas, Cuba

The boat reversed into the slip, and Young Mario skipped along the narrow gunwale and up to the bow. His long-handled gaff hook found the orange buoy, heavy with the wet weight of goose barnacles. Then he muscled the loop of the mooring line up over the Samson post.

Young Mario's life at sea had gifted him with supernatural balance and athletic speed. He made the work look easy as he pulled in both the stern lines and threw half hitches on the cleats. Then he tied off the spring lines that held the boat tight in its place.

He didn't notice that his Father had moved in from behind, until he swung around.

Mario Senior stood with his arms crossed. Then he gave his son, a hard look of anger. He grit his teeth down, on what was left of his cigar, his eyes on fire.

Young Mario quickly backed up a step or two. The mood for smiling vanished and his face fell into a worried look.

"What?" He waved his open hands. "What did I do now?" His

voice reached for a higher pitch as he looked around the deck for any little piece of unfinished work. "What did I forget to do?"

The father held his son in this state of anxiety for a long moment. Then he cooled his eyes to embers. The corner of his stern mouth began to quiver a bit, as it ever so slowly melted into a big, toothy grin. Then he chuckled in the same familiar tone of his son. He opened his arms and sang out two words. "Happy Birthday!"

Young Mario was greatly relieved to know that he didn't screw up and have to suffer through any lectures, or scolding. With only a slight hesitation, he entered into a stiff, manly, hug with his father.

"Hey, you didn't forget about my birthday. You were just holding out on me."

The father put his hands on the broad shoulders of one who was once his little boy. Now, he has to look up a bit to see him eye to eye. "Today is the day that the people will begin to call you a man. But I want you to know, that I have seen you this way for a long time now. I see it in the way you work, and in the love you show for your family. Today you have been alive for seventeen years, and now, you are that man."

The father walks away from his son, who is still standing with his chest puffed out, still hungry for more complements.

Mario Senior grabbed the stern line and pulled himself up onto the dock, then he turned to point at the deck, and said; "Hey Boy don't forget that bucket of grunts and junk fish." Then He offered up a gigantic, silly grin.

The head of Young Mario was swimming with all of his father's praise, but he still heard the word boy.

With a most indignant look, he pronounced, "Boy? Who are you calling a boy?" He said the word like it tasted rancid in his mouth. He poked his thumb into his chest, and said in a powerful voice; "This man is no longer a boy! And don't you ever forget it."

Then he aimed his finger like a pistol, at his much-amused Father.

Still trying to find some land legs, they took the coral rock steps up to the village and their modest home. So much alike, they appeared to be more like friends or brothers, rather than father and son. Along the way, they took turns punching each other, just like a couple of boys.

Soon they passed into the reach of a warm welcoming smell. When they neared the house, the air became thick with the fragrance of garlic and jungle oregano.

The two men stopped and looked at each other with wild eyes. They broke into a race, pushing and trying to trip each other, until they squeezed through the front door, together.

The fisherman's wife and their two little daughters had spent the day preparing a homecoming feast—spicy roast pork and fried sweet plantains. There was also a big steaming pot of Moro, a traditional dish of black beans and rice, cooked long and slow. The crust on the bottom was usually savored as a bed time snack.

When Mario Senior was full and satisfied with the wonderful woman-cooked meal. He leaned back in his rattan chair and closes his eyes, gratefully taking in the comfortable chatter at the family table.

But his mind began to stray to an old worry. One that he had quietly held inside for seventeen years: The mandatory military age for young men in Cuba.

CHAPTER 2
SHORTY

The black of the new-moon night erupted with an enormous thunder clap, shattering the silence and shaking the earth, followed by the static veins of white-hot fire that lit up the entire sky. The lightning illuminated the weather-worn buoy that leans with the wind chop of a quick-moving storm.

The instant also flashed on a crawfish boat, anchored fast against the wind and tide. It lay just inshore of the battered reef marker.

Gliding through the metallic smell of ozone and the sheeting rain, the Chip Chip was almost beaten. But her miracle did happen as she slipped invisibly under the canopy and landed in a dark corner behind a lobster trap. Finally a boat to survive with.

For a moment, she hopped from foot to foot, then spied a perfect perch. She jumped to a dry rafter in the open cabin, just above the sea clock. Then she tucked her head under her wing, and began to preen away the damage from her odyssey.

The cannonade of thunder sent a naked young Asian lady running from the stern and up into the same cabin. She flapped her arms and shivered from the cold rain. Shampoo streamed down her face. Her long hair was still coiled up on her head like soft serve ice cream.

Kim Sue was terrorized into a loss for words, but she could still make a lot of noise. "Oooche, Yobo! Ooooo Yoboo!. You come up-ee here, now…take-a me home, *now*!"

Out in the open on the back deck, Shorty was cool to the attack of the storm. He buried his neck between his shoulders, and rolled his gaze up to the low, black and breathing cloud. He refused the shelter of the cabin long enough for the rain to rinse the soap from his tall, lanky body.

The soft fresh water from under the storm provided them with an interesting shower, but his little girlfriend was cold and scared and she seemed to him, a silly sight. He grabbed an extra towel and, in no particular hurry, came to her rescue.

Customary to their relationship, he couldn't resist, teasing her. Usually the first goofy thing that popped in his head was enough to defuse some of her potential for a hissy fit. He put a surprised and stupid look on his face and, with a hillbilly voice, asked, "What's da matter, Honey Baby?"

Kim Sue's arms were crossed, and her legs went knock-kneed, trying for some warmth. Her teeth chattered as she yelled in broken English, "Help me Yobbo, I cold, I very cold."

So he picked up a plastic jug of cool, fresh water and slowly poured it over her head. Her long straight hair emerged from the suds moving down over her scrunched up face and shoulders.

"Hurry, Yobbo, hurry!"

Shorty took his good time and grinned like a mischievous kid as he opens another jug and finished rinsing her off. Then he gently hugged her with a fresh, towel. As he dried her, he admired her slight but pretty body, and then he said, "Damn, we're lucky. That lightning hit the buoy, and I do believe a branch of it might've tickled the boat a little. Let me tell ya. A head on strike would have made us look like a couple of fried shrimp."

As she warmed to the towel and regained her vocabulary, she plowed into her boyfriend, who just happened to be more than twice her size.

"No, no, you big monster, you would look like a big burnt lobster and I, I would look like a fried shrimp!"

Within a few minutes she broke a little smile and ended her demands to go home. His grin turned into a comfortable smile.

Kim Sue made a bed on the engine box, still warm from the turbo engine down below. The squall had passed, just as quickly as it appeared. Shorty made a last check of the boat before they lay down. It was a proper habit to know the boat's condition. More often than not, the extra effort will prevent any breakdowns in the middle of nowhere. He looked over the side as he pulled the switch for the bilge pump and watched the oily water being purged into the sea. Then he added a stream of his own, while his eyes followed a green running light in the distance.

He joined Kim Sue in the nest she made. As he spooned up to her, she swished him back. "Oh, no, Shorty, not again."

He pouted for a second or two and then rolled over and into a quick, but shallow sleep.

挀&#x80

People become an unnatural presence when they took themselves out to sea. They had entered the last great wilderness, a whole other world. With lungs and limbs instead of gills and fins, and without the gift of wings, people survived by the grace of the boat beneath them.

Seagoing folks who reached a ripe age had more than just luck in their pocket. They were the ones who remembered to respect the abiding unknown, which defined the great oceans of the world.

In the Caribbean, thousands of islands and complicated waterways had given that sea a brightly-colored history. For five centuries it had been the crossroads of shipping between Europe, Africa and the Americas. Man's law had little reach in such a vast place. The unseen potential of the natural elements would always try the bravest, and bring them to their knees.

But it's the lower nature of mankind that brought the worst danger. A dangerous breed hid just over the horizon. Always waiting, and always ready to challenge the innocent or unaware.

The privateers and salvagers of history were nightmares to earlier generations.

In modern times, it was smugglers, who traded guns for drugs and dabbled in white slavery.

A few stories are always making the rounds at the docks.

A sleeping boat would be boarded, and the crew overcome. There would be no offer to join the modern-day pirates. Only a wicked, screaming death to be silenced by the depths. The vessel would be used for the dirty business, then scuttled. No evidence to be found. Just another report of a missing boat.

But in the end, the fear and exhilaration of working on the ocean made for a life fantastic, and better lived than most.

Rather than sleep soundly down below in the bunks, Shorty chose the engine box. It was the true center of the boat and he could easily sit up and take notice of any sound different from the waves lapping at the hull.

It was usually just the spout of a porpoise, or the exhale of a loggerhead turtle.

But there were times when a being a wary sleeper paid for the fatigue.

Still fresh in Shorty's memory was a night when he rose to the hum of large engines. The adrenalin ran hot in his veins when he looked up to the freighter bearing down on him. The ship had cut its course too close to the reef, and had little concern for anything in its path.

He had run up to the bow with his upswept bait knife and cut the anchor rope. He had cranked the motor up, and threw the throttle down in order to wheel his way from under the fast-moving wall of steel.

He had to shake off the sickening shock and handle his boat through the great wake behind the towering ship.

When he had settled into the wash, he drifted and stared at the hulk until it became distant lights, disappearing into the dark curved horizon. He hugged his knees, and took in a long breath that caught a few times in his throat.

Then he had raised his arms, and tossed back his sandy-haired head to see the whole sky. His blue-gray eyes were enlightened as he proclaimed for all the earth to hear; "Dear God, I promise, and I really mean it this time, I *will* start going to church again!"

CSSO

The pinks and blues began to crawl across the slick, calm water as the sky in the east gains the gold of a new day.

Shorty was already standing at the small galley and its two-burner gas stove. He was loading the espresso pot with the rich black coffee they called Buche. His mouth hung open, waiting for a long yawn.

The thick, syrupy caffeine had the effect of liquid speed. Just a few small shots would prop open the eyes of any tired person.

He had risen from his sleep no less than a dozen times. The distant sounds of boat motors invaded his dreams. It was unusual, he thought, that more than just a few would anchor on this part of the reef. He had tried the VHF radio, but could only get a useless hum from the lightning damage.

Just as he turned to see the sunrise, a school of flying fish launched from the silvery, purple water. Their tails skipped across the mirrored surface. With enough speed, they entered the air gliding in random order and leaving behind a big swirl at the surface.

A confused and frustrated Barracuda decided to hang along the side for a while.

Shorty heard a flapping at the stern. So he carefully walked past the sound sleeping, and slightly snoring, Kim Sue. He put his cup of coffee on the gunwale and gently picked up the glass-like fish that had landed on the back deck.

It looked small in his hand as he examined the beautiful, transparent life form. He pulleds its peck fin out to reveal the wing that allowed it to escape its many predators. He went to release it, but noticed that the great barracuda was still on the starboard. So he walked to the other side and carefully placed the glass fish back into the water. He watched for its recovery, and was relieved when it darted away.

♋

Shorty had the look of a lover of everything natural and this was exactly how he saw himself, a student of life who was always hungry to fill his senses with more. He knew he was lucky to have fallen into this new world and the opportunity to work on the ocean.

It offered many things to ponder and explore. Perfect for a man who could easily become bored.

He had arrived in the Florida Keys a few years earlier, a refugee from the Rust Belt in the upper Midwest. A typical working-class kid, whose only experience with boats had been in a canoe on a pond.

Like many young people in those days, he had traveled via his thumb looking for work, looking for a life, which he believed he finally found in the Keys.

It wasn't easy for someone who didn't grow up around the water. Shorty had to develop a set of big ones in order to muscle his way into this business. You had to be born in the Lower Keys and call yourself a Conch to safely enter the commercial fishing docks. The locals who had ruled these waters for many generations were always leery of outsiders.

The growing popularity of tourism in Key West had given success to some, and ruin to others. To the diehard Conchs, anyone who came from north of Marathon Key was considered a Damn Yankee.

Because of that, in the beginning Shorty had to prove his cool to the tough, young brotherhood of crawfishermen. He made himself learn fast, and before long, he could outwork the best among them. Now he was the trusted first mate on a forty-five foot lobster boat, with well over a thousand traps to maintain. Most of the guys had grown to trust, and even like, the thoughtful and honest-talking Northerner. He was someone who preferred having a good day, over a bad one.

Crawfish boats were custom-made for average-sized men to work on. Shorty was just too tall to avoid banging his head on the low hanging doors and devices, leaving knots on top of knots on his poor skull. The use of self-deprecating humor helped him laugh off the sharp, burning, pains. Often he would say things like, "Ah, that felt real good" or "Maybe that will knock some sense into me."

He was carved hard from the body breaking work of pulling more than three hundred traps a day. He also took a double share for doing the work of two men.

The money was a good thing, but he seemed to work better alone. He found himself tripping over the other mates who couldn't keep up with the pace.

The traps were pulled weekly in order to keep them in the best shape and the most productive. They needed to be scraped of the barnacles and razor oysters that grow quickly on the wooden slats. Fresh flags, made of raw bull hide pieces, were suspended by wire inside each one. These would gradually melt in the sea water, and attract the spiny lobster to the shelter on the bottom.

The crawfish were quickly pulled through the funnel, and tossed over the shoulder to the sorting crates behind.

It was part of Shorty's morning routine to thaw his swollen, salt-dried hands in warm fresh water. When he could open, and close them once again, they oozed from the many cuts and punctures from the bait wires and lobster spines.

But the work, was so fascinating that he had become one with his job and numb to the nuisance of pain. Injuries and hangovers went unnoticed and he absorbed it all, as part of feeling alive.

⊗⊗⊘

Kim Sue woke to her own morning, a bit annoyed to find herself still on this offshore camping trip with her fiancé.

Cheerfully Shorty greeted her into the day, by saying; "Cafe, cafe con leche for my sweet, and hopefully, happy lady?"

Her voice went into a complaint mode. "When are you gonna build a real bathroom on this dirty damn boat?"

Shorty bowed to her needs and handed her a bucket with a rope handle. The name "John" was painted in red on its side. With a serious look, he told her; "Now go have some fun."

She grabbed it begrudgingly and cursed at him in Korean making her way behind the fish box. As she dipped a few inches of sea water into the makeshift toilet, she gives Shorty an evil look and then growls at him.

He loved her animated kookiness and always exaggerated his fear of her, so he said; "OK, OK just don't bite me, please."

With one hand, he lifted the big engine cover, and leaned it on the gunwale. Then he jumped down into the bilge to check the fluids of the massive motor. As he stood next to the freshly-painted green engine, he raised his voice a notch to carry over to Kim Sue. "Hey did you see all the boats anchored along the reef?

From her seat on the bucket she looked up over the side, to the east. With a puzzled look taking over the pout on her face she said; "Wow, that's really weird Yobbo. Why do you think they're so many? Did you hear anything on the radio?"

"Naa. That lightning strike did a number on the antenna. I've been up all night trying to figure it all out. Looks to me like a bunch are heading south. Just like this one here."

He watched the approaching shrimp boat with its loud clanging outriggers. It passed within fifty yards of their anchored boat.

Shorty closed the engine cover and cleaned his hands with a rag. Then he wiped the sweat from his forehead with his shoulder, and said, "Damn, I wish I knew what was going on. Maybe it has something to do with Cuba." Then he called out to Kim Sue, "Hey, when you get done there, please see if you can dig out that old boom box down below. We need some news. Oh, yeah, by the way, you better find something to hang onto. The wake from that Shrimper is gonna hit us broadside. Right about...."

He hesitated a second for Kim Sue to heed the warning, but she was too slow to react.

"...now!"

She looked up, arms folded around her knees, just as the boat roses up and rolled with the big, wave. Her bucket took off on the wet, slippery deck and slid from one side to the other. Her little feet stepped quickly to keep up with her seat.

As Shorty prepared to pull in the rock anchor, he heard her vibrating voice.

"Woo....weoo!"

He acted content with her effort to not spill the bucket. Then he cautiously teased her by saying; "Nice job."

Of course, she didn't think it was funny at all. After dumping and rinsing the toilet, she threw it at him. He covered his head as he prepared himself for the belligerent assault from his little panther girl, then laughed and slapped down the bucket. Then he tried to appear sympathetic.

She ignored him with a rude face as she passed him by on her way to the cabin to clean up.

With a cautious voice he said, "I've got some good news for you."

"Good news?" she flashed back at him. "What good news could come from a big…" She paused for a second to find the right word. "…gorilla like you?"

Shorty broke into a laugh that resonated from his belly and said, "We're going in. There's no sense in being out here another day or two without a radio."

Still a little perturbed with the potty experience, she said, "Good!"

Then she slammed the hatch shut behind her and went below to change.

Shorty throttled down and broke loose the anchor, then put it in neutral. He ran back with a gaff hook and pulled in on the anchor rope. It coiled neatly at his feet. He lay the chain and big grapple across it, as if they were weightless.

The old familiar skyline of Key West rose up and out of the sea before them. The couple appeared to be the only ones heading into the port. The ships channel was busy with hundreds of vessels of every type. They were all leaving their dockage and heading south.

One of the distant boats, looking like a tiny white dot on the horizon, appeared to turn inshore towards them.

Shorty told Kim Sue, "Look honey, that's Jerry. It looks like he is heading this way to talk."

She squinted, then turned a befuddled look at him. "How can you tell that's Jerry's boat from this far away?"

"I don't know, I guess after a while we just know each other's boats."

CRBO

Friends of necessity, the brotherhood of crawfishermen was familiar with the profiles of each other's similar-looking boats.

Wound up tight and fiercely competitive, they would race to keep their lines of traps in front of the migrating spiny lobster. Little wars would break out, often among lifelong friends. For many it was more than just temptation to steal an easy harvest from the traps and hard work of another fisherman. It could quickly become a dangerous game.

A common phrase around the docks was, "If you snooze, you lose," a friendly but sinister warning to stay on top of your gear. Retaliation for this almost-acceptable greed could be the cutting away of many valuable handmade traps. At times the battles could escalate and spill over onto the docks. The yellow crime scene tape was a familiar sight around the fish house.

A sleek, fiberglass hull could burn right to the water line. When blood dries in the sun on the crushed coral parking lot, it would look no different than an oil stain, to be walked around.

A popular phrase was, "Don't get mad, get even." An early experience for Shorty was either a warning, or just a welcome to the way it was out there.

One time he thought a trap he was pulling looked kind of strange as it cleared the water. When he slammed it down on the gunwale, a rotten, bloated Pelican exploded in his face. The rancid liquids of the rotting flesh ran down his oilers and into his boots.

Someone he knew, probably a friend, a regular Smiling Jack, had stuffed it in his trap a few days earlier.

In a world of people who make a living by harvesting the ocean, any show of weakness could put you out of business.

A barroom conversation with a couple of the guys lead him to the culprit.

So the next time out Shorty went on a scavenger hunt, he pulled eighty traps that belonged to the so-called friend. He broke the slats on each one, so that they could no longer fish, and sent them all to the bottom.

The ropes were cut off and kept. He would use them on his own traps, to save on the expense of buying new. Shorty left them nicely coiled on his deck for a week, so that everyone could see.

A little warning of his own.

But, in the long run, if one of the brothers found themselves in deep shit, whether it was with the hostile ocean or in a rough-and-tumble shrimper bar downtown, they would somehow show up, and then cover each other's back.

CRBO

As the two lobster boats grew closer, it became like a game of chicken.

Just as they reached the brink of a head-on, each man cut his wheel to the right and throttled down into a counter circle. They dropped it in reverse to stop side by side, in opposing directions.

As they took turns rising and falling in each other's wake, the two young men slid open the cabin windows and swiveled around in their cushioned captain's chairs.

Compelled to act macho and cool in each other's presence, they both appeared nonchalant and seemed bored with it all.

Shorty yawned and hung out his window. With an exaggerated voice he asked; "What de hail is goin' on 'round here?"

Then he looked down at the water and spit.

Jerry pulled off his Ray Bans and cleaned a lens with the corner of his shirt.

"Ah," he said, "not too much. Just a couple of thousand boats goin' to Cuba, that's all."

He shifted his eyes over to the Holy Shit look on Shorty's face. Then he asked, "Hey, bubba, what's with your radio?"

Shorty shrugged and said, "Antenna got fried last night. It's no biggie. What's with this Cuba thing?"

Jerry explained "Same shit happened when I was a kid. We had the Bay of Pigs. It won't be long before all them boats will be headin' back, loaded down with Cubans."

He said the last word with a little animosity.

Shorty quickly asked, "Are you going?"

"Nah," Jerry said. "Momma don't want either of her boats to get in the middle of what's gonna be a big mess. My brother and me are gonna sit this one out."

"Damn. Do you think Dagger plans on sending me down there?"

Jerry looked Shorty in the eye. "Most probably."

Then the Tarantula tattoo on his forearm moved with the flex as he put his boat in gear. He began to idle away, then turned and hollered back to Shorty. "You be careful down there."

Shorty put on his brave-it-all look and quickly changed the subject. "Hey, bubba, looks like you're headed to Monkey Jungle." Then he beams a knowing smile.

Jerry gave him a wicked and greedy laugh, then rubbed his thumb and forefinger together and said, "Yeah, I think I'll head over that way and see if I can't pick up a Few Stragglers."

Monkey Jungle was an area in the Shallows in front of Man Key and Woman Key. It was infested with the easy to catch, but illegal to possess, undersized lobster. Most of the fishermen would defy the searches of the Marine Patrol by hiding bags of the small lobster tails they called "monkeys" deep in the bilges of their boats. They sold for a good price and became a little black market bonus. One that typically went fast in Party Town, USA.

CRED

As Kim Sue and Shorty neared the channel of Safe Harbor, the fast work boat cut through the sweet land perfume.

The speedy scent raised the tiny bird from its hidden perch. It flew, confused, around the cabin and then between the couple. She landed on one of the traps at the stern, buzzing with a strange energy.

The sudden flight startled the couple. It snagged their worried attention away from the creepy vacuum of the commercial fishing docks.

"Oooh, Yobbo, look at the pretty birdie!"

Then she followed it with her finger out.

Shorty smiled and shook his head, knowing that the wild bird would never let her close.

Then, proud with his natural knowledge, he said; "That little land bird is called a Chip Chip. She joined us last night, out on the reef, during that pisser of a squall. People say they bring good luck to a boat. Watch her, she's probably going to take off and head back offshore. It's weird that they do that, with all these islands to live on."

As they passed the no-wake sign, Shorty throttled down and asked Kim Sue to take the wheel for a few minutes.

He looked over the side to make sure the bilge pump was working. Then he walked to the stern to check the exhaust. As he climbed onto the traps, Shorty spoke softly to the bird, just like it was a fearful friend. "Go on now. Go do your thing."

The Chip Chip launched her ounce of life into the shore breeze and flew straight into infinite sea.

Then Shorty smiled at Kim Sue and said, "See what I mean?"

CHAPTER 3
LAID BACK AND STRANGE

The Chip Chip had borne her way several miles into the void of the ocean when a swirl of scented air lifted her up from behind.

The land air was like a wonderful soup of many smells. Her tiny mind dissected this air until she tasted one particular scent buried deep in the others. She decided against her own instincts and made a long, wide turn back toward the land.

The Chip Chip would make a quick reunion with a gnarly old Poinciana tree that overlooked Duval street. She landed on the same branch that once saw her tumble and glide into her first flight.

At first, the busy noise of the crowded sidewalk below aroused a nervous chip, chipping, and sent her into agitated hops.

She blurred it all out and hid in her circle of awareness. Then she leaned into the crook of the tree. Only her head would dart around to each of the sharper sounds nearby.

Peddling briskly on a Conch cruiser bicycle, a tall, lovely young lady turned onto the side street and glided under the great old tree. The cyclist was in a trance. She wore only a long transparent silk gown, and had Rapunzel-like hair that streamed in her own breeze.

At the top of her lungs she sang the pure notes of opera. Then she disappeared into the bubbles and back streets

Directly under the branch was a gray-haired, tattooed arm working a paint brush. The top of his old sailor's cap was yellow and gray. The old street artist stepped back to admire the fresh paint covering the canvas. As he wiped his hands on a cloth, he smiled at passersby, hoping for a sale.

After a few moments, he resigned his slow body to a worn-out, fragile lawn chair. Next to one of his flip flops was a rusted coffee can salted with a few greenbacks. Occasionally he stroked it with his big toe.

Five dog leashes looped around his other ankle, each one attached to a very large, and very still, Iguana. Some were deep shades of green, the others a weird orange and florescent brown.

Sprawled around him, they appeared laid back and strange. No different than many of the human residents of Key West

In 1980, the island city was wide open. It was the end of the line. The Southernmost point in the U.S.A. There was only one road in and it was the same road out. Close to a hundred and fifty miles into the emerald green and sky-blue ocean. It perched on the only living reef that was part of the Continental United States. Without needing a boat, anyone could drive the many spans of bridges to get there. It had always been remote, and distant from the mainstream life that existed elsewhere. Far from those who, for the most part, lived by the rules.

One of the working parts of the famous island city was the street people.

Forever, the small island had welcomed into its fold, many people who seemed to be the farthest from normal. It was a haven for individualists to be comfortable, and free to be strange.

To be different was to be normal, in a novel town like Key West.

It also played a welcoming host to runaways and homeless, who appeared from the cracks and crannies at first light of each day. They claimed their spots and set up for the day of panhandling. An acceptable trade and sometimes very lucrative.

One played a drum set made of cans and junk from a dumpster. Another sold handmade key chains or shell necklaces. A banjo case opened up on the sidewalk held a pile of accumulated loose change. Standing behind it was a hungry-looking kid playing bluegrass riffs. A few were very young and appeared to come from damaged backgrounds. Some sold their bodies, and likewise their souls, for the only kind of love they had ever known.

Every day, this ever-changing and diverse group of persons reinvented the circus, which was the enchanting allure of the town.

The many tourists easily paid tribute to the street performers. Money flowed free in exchange for the experience of Key West.

The true locals were the Conchs, who perhaps representing the only real normalcy. They either worked the boats or they ran the unique small businesses that could only be found there.

Every other storefront was either a restaurant or a bar, with live acoustic music and Caribbean flavors spilling out and over the streets.

Most every day, Key West looked like a Spring Break destination. Pink ladies who were looking for a quick tan. Young men with New England accents drinking warm beer in the tropical sun and bragging about their conquests. Families on vacation, who bought tee shirts by the armfuls, and tried to keep track of their children in the crowds. There was always a parade of tour buses full of retirees wearing their brightest colors and visiting on the tightest budgets.

The Sunset at Malory Square was a celebration for the gift of another day. The big orange sun in the sky would sink below the line of the horizon. Everyone was amazed how quickly it disappeared into the Ocean. When it was finally gone, leaving only fiery rays in the west, there was thundering applause. Then everyone returned to Main Street and continued with the Celebration.

At night, the air was layered with the feathering scent of night blooming jasmine. The fragrance weaved through the brick court yards and floated randomly through the walking crowds.

The warmth of the tropics aroused the sensuality of most everyone, even the most prudent. Inventive drinks of liquor were served and created the kind of sweat that subconsciously draws people together.

Most evenings had the feel of Mardi Gras. Everyone was invited to cut loose and behave in a fresh new way—a way that many would try to forget about the next day.

But there was a deep, almost black, side to such a fascinating place. Con artists and thieves blended into the crowds who were entranced with the bright and fun times. Crime was quiet and almost invisible. But it was there, seeking out anyone who seemed vulnerable.

At every turn of a street, and throughout the alleyways, choking with vegetation, was the faint smell of history.

Key West was often called by its original name, Cayo Hueso, which meant the Island of Bones.

Some of the most savage, and then again some of the sweetest, events had happened on the Island. Most of the past seemed forgotten, but it could be felt when someone stood on the sand of this small patch of land in the middle of the sea.

Hundreds of years had passed under watchful eyes of the gnarly old Poinciana tree. As long as it stood, the old history, good and bad, would linger, and the future would have some shade to be born into.

From a back yard cafe came a loud burst of laughter. The sharp human noise sent the Chip Chip into the sky once more. The old tree offered to give rest to the fragile little bird. But the stress of so much human commotion sapped her energy.

Once again, she was free, sailing the air. After circling a few times, she hitched a ride on a southerly wind. The Chip Chip tuned to that singular voice that only she could hear. It softly called her to face the north.

The gentile fingers of nature caressed her back into the void. Then she entered into the vast emptiness of the Gulf of Mexico.

CHAPTER 4
DAGGER'S FISH HOUSE

The eyes of Kim Sue and Shorty opened wide as they turned into the basin the lobster boats called home. They had never seen the fish house as busy as it was that morning. Typically, the cinder block building and its concrete dock saw a working speed. Usually just a boat, or two at a time, with a steady transfer of fish, and ice.

Now, more than a hundred excited and emotional people, mostly from Miami, swarmed around the weighting scales and block the front of the walk-in cooler. Camera crews pushed their way through the crowd, following behind the sniffing and hungry lenses.

Shorty glided the boat alongside the chained tires that hung on the seawall. Without touching the dock, he backed down to stop.

A leathery bulldog of a man stepped out from the herd of strangers and tossed a rope up to the front. Then he stepped on board and helped Kim Sue tie off the stern line.

Shorty's long legs took just three strides along the gunwale to the bow, where he quickly lashed the rope.

Dagger smiled at Kim Sue and mumbled something off-color, but probably very funny.

As he went up into the cabin to shut his motor down, he glared at Shorty and said, "God damn, Chiquitico, Where the hell ya been with my boat?"

Then he turned an aggravated glance over to the annoying swarm of strangers who surrounded his fish house.

Shorty was even tempered and had a long fuse, but he took his work seriously. So he spit right back at his captain, who was also a bit of his father figure.

"Hey, man. I couldn't wake your drunk ass up, so I took it upon myself to go out and rescue some more of **your** gear. I damn sure don't want to build new traps all summer."

The crusty old World War II veteran liked to get a rise out of the big, young Yankee. So he said, "Calm down. Calm down there, Shorty. What's a matter, don't you put your radio on anymore?"

"Naw. I think the antenna got frazzled by a little lightning, That's why I'm in so early."

Dagger looked at the dozen traps stacked neatly at the stern. "Is that all you got for me?"

Shorty took a long breath. "The tide was rippin' out there on that deep water set. Most of the floats were pulled under, so I grappled up what I could see. I figure it will let up after this next moon and we can go back out and find them."

Then he added, "We can't forget about those two short strings that we left in Boca Grande Channel."

Dagger's serious business face popped into a broad smile. "Gimme five, Bro."

Thinking it was a congratulatory hand shake for a job well done, Shorty gave him a firm grab of the hand. Then he lifte his blond eyebrows and opened his hand to see a thick wad of hundred dollar bills. He quickly shoved it into his pocket and looked Dagger square in the eyes for the reason.

A news camera edged around the high-pitched noise of the commotion. It began filming the boat. Then it honed in on the dock employees who were unloading Shorty's catch of live lobster and iced fish. When the Cameraman panned over to the cabin, Dagger waved him on, with an intimidating, hard look.

Kim Sue jumped in front of the camera, smiling and waving. Smiling and waving at who knows who. But she managed to divert the attention away from the captain and his first mate, who had entered into a serious conversation.

Shorty walked over to the dock side, with pressed lips and studying eyes. After a minute, he shook his head and turned to his captain and asked the obvious question. "So what's with all this crap I'm hearin' about Cuba?"

❧

Dagger was a tough but personable old guy. The young brotherhood of lobster men always called him the General. He was the respected pioneer of the thriving spiny lobster industry in the Florida Keys. A true Key West character and well known not only around the docks, but also downtown.

But recent years had seen him lay back with a young, half-crazy girl who changed his course. He had to reinforce his strength with Spanish Brandy, and what he called Peruvian Marching Powder.

He was no longer the top producer, or as they said around the docks, High Hooker, nor did he really seem to care much. After a war in the Pacific, and thirty long years of the bone-crushing work that comes with commercial fishing, Dagger was ready to retire and allow the good times to roll.

This gave Shorty a chance to show some incentive by picking up the slack. He quietly aspired to someday become one of the Key West captains and have a long career as a professional fisherman. It was not an easy endeavor, so he dove on every chance to gain some experience, and also, to prove himself.

If he couldn't raise his captain to work, he would take Kim Sue to drive the boat as he pulled the traps. It was slower than the power team of Dagger and Shorty, but it worked well enough.

Most of the capable mates were in solid employment, and on the best-producing boats. This only leaves a few drunks and junkies hanging around the docks looking for day work. They were a liability around the dangerous mechanics of harvesting lobster.

Shorty preferred not using these types of men, and refereed to them as Burnt Spoons.

❧

"Look, don't say nuttin', jest listen." Dagger waved Shorty over to explain. "These people are desperate to go to Cuba. They want to bring back their families and friends, and they're willing to pay anything for a boat ride. Make no mistake. This is a big deal, and there's a ton of money to be had. We could be bringing people back here every week for months."

He nodded to the wad of cash that bulged in Shorty's pocket.

Shorty says; "Does that mean I gotta go with you?"

Dagger laughed. "No, I mean **your** ass is gonna go. I'm staying here to take care of business."

Shorty was usually game for just about any excursion that might place him on the edge of the world. But he was still a little cool to the thought of going into a Communist country. "Wouldn't that be breaking some sort of immigration laws? That shit's federal. It would be a real bite in the ass to jeopardize this boat."

"Don't fret about it. Ole Jimmy Carter said on the news, open heart, open arms. I'd say, Bring em on over."

Both men were pumped up with the prospect of making some fast money. But Dagger had a real soft spot for the Cuban people who rot just ninety miles away. His late wife had been born and raised there, and he himself had a strong Cuban heritage.

He cherished many good memories of the island country back when it was still free. Like most Cuban Americans, he hated Castro. Whenever he heard the name, his fists would ball up and his anger reached the surface. He often made comments like; "I'd love to give that bastard a little lead pill.

Dagger pointed over to the crowd around his fish house. "See that couple over there by the cooler door? Right there, next to the pay phone?"

Shorty nodded and watched the middle-aged Cuban-American wife and husband.

"That's Felicia and Eduardo Fernandez. They chartered my boat and have a list of four family members to request, once you get settled down there."

"What? Those people are going with me? Hell, we don't even have a damn toilet on board. What da hell am I gonna do with a couple of whiny-assed tourists on a trip like this?"

Dagger had a quick answer, "How the hell are you gonna find their people without them? Besides, they can translate for you."

Shorty knew more Spanish than he would let on. He had a lot of fun with a surprising fluency in Cuban cuss words. But he knew that Dagger was right. He would be in a place where a small miscommunication could cause a big problem. But he was still hesitant about taking any Land Crabs across the Straits of Florida. It could be a rough piece of water for the inexperienced.

Dagger grinned. "That's not all. See the older lady next to them? That's Esperanza Sanchez. She's going to look for her twin sister and two nieces."

Shorty scrunched up his face, his hand on his head. He turned to his laughing Captain. "I can't believe you're doing this shit to me." Then he shook his head, and with a suspicious tone, asked, "Is all this written in stone?"

Dagger laughed at Shorty, who was still trying to digest the situation. "I'm gonna send these good people to pick up about ten days' worth of groceries. How many cases of beer do you need?"

Shorty could never say no to his captain, so he resigned himself to take the boat where it needs to go. He held up both hands to show ten fingers, to make sure he had an overstock of beer. Then he went quiet and began to prepare his brain for this questionable journey.

Dagger said "I'm gonna run down to the Marine Hardware and pick up a new antenna for the radio. Now, go be a gentleman and introduce yourself to your new passengers. Then I want you to fuel up and top off the ice. Make sure you carry plenty of fresh water."

Dagger snapped Shorty out of his fleet of thoughts and said with a growl, "You just make damn sure you don't lose my boat, down there."

The serious tone of that command sent the chill of a dangerous reality right up the back of the young man's neck. Flooding with uncertainty, his head swam as he looked to the South.

Then he became flushed with adrenalin, and it fluttered down to his stomach. Excitement took over as he prepared for the onset of a new adventure.

CHAPTER 5
GAFF HOOK

A gentle Southwest breeze joined with the Gulf Stream and lay the seas down into a soft swell. A good-sized pod of porpoise stayed with the boat for most of the comfortable crossing. Hitching a ride on the wake, they took turns winning or losing little races with the boat. The winners would skyrocket, drilling the air, as they spin across the bow, much to the delight of the Passengers.

Shorty was alone in the fly bridge and had been driving the boat for ten hours. The human-like sea creatures were common to his life. He never grew tired of enjoying their friendship.

There had been a last-minute add-on to the group. A tall, thin man who went by the name Flaco.

When Shorty first met Flaco, the hair stood up on the back of his neck. Long ago he had learned that his instincts could be as valuable as any logic. He always believed in what he could feel.

Back at the dock, Dagger tried to convince Shorty that Flaco had some experience on the ocean, and could help with the boat. He also had a list of four friends of his own that he wanted to retrieve from Cuba.

Shorty gave the old captain a quick and calm response. "I don't need any help. Don't you worry, I'll take good care of your boat myself."

They weren't even half way across and this arrogant man had already challenged the compass bearing that Shorty had set.

Shorty's dead reckoning was always right on. He took the time to allow for the wind and tide before he would plot a course.

He knew he had to remain patient with the patronizing smile and know-it-all attitude, which seemed to come with Flaco. The boat wasn't very big and with two opposing personalities sharing the same space, a little time together is bound to show a big problem.

In contrast, Shorty was flattered with the respect and admiration that the other three passengers had shown him. They were lighthearted and excited with the hope of soon seeing their loved ones.

Shorty promised himself to maintain the peace on the boat.

His thoughts drift between the new, unknown experience that lies ahead, and his tiny girlfriend back home. Whenever his mind went back in her direction, a hollowness filled his midsection. He knew that he was probably a little too insecure, and way too possessive with her. But it was the first time that he ever played house with a girl.

Shorty left her with most of the cash, but it wasn't the money that worried him.

Kim Sue had a way of keeping him on the edge of jealousy, and frustration. She loved to dance and was a regular in every disco club in the area. Men were drawn to her exotic cuteness, and she had no qualms about being flirtatious. Many times, this behavior had burned his feelings of forever with her. As a couple, they were a popular novelty around Key West. He was built like a linebacker and she looked like a little girl standing next to him. It was truly a case of opposites attracting each other. Hot breath and sweat would make stream rise from their bed. But when it came to conversation and interaction as a couple, they found little common ground. Even with her decent command of English, they rarely understood each other. There was a gap between the two cultures. One that only love could fill. A love that he wasn't really sure of.

Even in a town that was full of beautiful, willing women, many of whom would love to be with the big, nice guy, Shorty was determined to make things work with his Miss Right, and remained good old-fashioned, true blue.

He was hoping to his very core that she was doing the same.

CঙৎO

The coastline of Cuba was becoming clear, and closer. The sight gave the young man a big tinge of goose bumps.

He could see an ancient Spanish fort carved from the rocks overlooking the mouth of Mariel Harbor. Always fascinated with history, he wondered what role the fortress and its long black cannons had played, back in the pirate days.

Outside of the inlet, a good number of boats drifted, waiting for an escort to lead them into the Harbor. Shorty recognized the familiar shapes of three other crawfish boats. So he adjusted his course a few degrees to join them.

As he came close, the sandalwood scent of fine Colombian smoke washed across his face. It raised a smile.

Five guys from his fish house were gathered together in the fly bridge of the bigger boat. It made him feel that at least he wouldn't be alone, or without allies, on this worrisome trip.

From under the shade of the Bimini top a big, hairy arm waves to Shorty, inviting him over to the loud, impromptu party.

Yogie was a stout, dark man with bristling black hair and beard. His ice blue and terminally bloodshot eyes had a way of looking right through a man. Whether he was happy and content or angry as a guard dog, Captain Yogie always showed a brilliant smile. The older captain had a gutsy reputation and was the unofficial leader of the young brotherhood of crawfishermen. He was also a longtime friend and partner with Dagger.

A few of the more clannish Conchs hadn't warmed up to the big Yankee yet, but Yogie had taken a liking to him early on. Yogie knew how powerful Shorty was, at working the deck. He also realized that it took some serious balls for the Yankee to break into this business. Once he even offered Shorty a bigger share if he would come over to work on his boat. But Shorty remained loyal to Dagger, which gained him even more respect.

Shorty pulled alongside the fifty-four footer. Then he tapped it into reverse to keep the two boats from hitting each other. He jumped down on the bow to wait for the right roll to make his leap.

He turned and gave a polite smile and a wave to his curious passengers. Then he climbed up to the noisy group of fishermen on the big crawfish boat.

The energetic conversation was driven by many ice cold beers. Along with a ridiculous number of fat joints. There was a unanimous excitement about the prospects of making the big bucks. The lobster season would be over now for the next sixteen weeks. Paychecks would become thin, and far between. Hand lining yellow tail snapper would be fun work, and provide a little income. But nothing like the more lucrative lobster.

So many joints were being passed around that they lost track of which way to pass them. Just as Shorty put one in Yogie's hand, his mate passed one to his other. The bristly captain made a comical, cross-eyed look, as he pinched a doobie in each hand. Then he snorted a laugh full of smoke from his nostrils.

He passed the joint on, held up his hands and said, "Enough."

Then he let his face go serious and patiently waited for the younger men to notice he had something to say. When they grew silent, he started to speak in a low voice.

"You guys know we ain't supposed to carry guns or drugs into that harbor."

They were shocked into total quiet for a second or two. Then they put the party back on, thinking that he was just bullshitting them. These guys wouldn't go anywhere without their essentials, and could never imagine feeling that naked.

But Shorty knew Yogie was for real and reached down to feel the fresh bag of buds he had stashed in his sock.

Yogie took on a sober tone and raised his voice above the others. "Hey, we're going into a damn Communist country, and they have a bunch of rules that we ain't used to."

Then he pulled a stainless steel Bulldog from behind his shirt. This very quickly regained everyone's attention. They all knew that it was his favorite little big gun. As he held it over the side, Yogie really enjoyed the stunned look on all of their faces. Then without a care he dropped the expensive weapon into the ocean.

Shorty knew that Yogie had a great stash spot hidden somewhere deep in the bilge of the big boat. It had foiled many searches from the Marine Patrol looking for Monkeys, or other contraband. He was sure that the older captain had more than just a few serious weapons hidden away. He realized this was just a show, so Shorty decided to go next and turn this into some sort of ritual sacrifice.

He stood up and opened the bag of weed and started shaking it out into the water. At the last second, he snatched one big bud and puts it in the cellophane wrapper from a pack of smokes. As he pushed it into his pocket he told the watching men, "Hell, I'll eat it if I have to," then smiled a stoned smile.

While he was still standing, he made the chatter fade behind his back. He turned to scan some more of the coastline of a country that was new to him. Shorty understood that the unknown is the Mother of all Fear. He had a healthy habit of taking a good, long look at whatever scared him.

Cuba appeared to be a truly beautiful place. He liked the way the rich, green mountains seemed to flow down into the deep blue water. He also took note of the smooth, silver trunks of the bottle-shaped Royal Palms that dotted the country side.

Years of fishing had trained his eyes to grab onto any slight difference on the ocean surface. He shifted his sight to a patch of water halfway between the old fort and the drifting boats. He put his hands above his brow, tried to find the small splash among the white caps that caught his eye.

There it was again, just a slight uneven texture to the water. It was a good distance away. A cold rush ran up his backbone as he began to make out a swimmer nearly a mile out from the jetty.

Yogie noticed Shorty straining to see something. "Conjo, Chiquitico What the hell ya lookin' at?"

Then he stood to see for himself.

Shorty turned and said, "Hey man, put me on my boat."

As soon as he was behind the wheel, he laid down the throttle and coursed to where he last saw the desperate swimmer.

One with the moment, he had forgotten about his passengers down below. They were almost slammed down to the deck, but were able to hold on. He never heard Yogie calling out to get his attention and pointing over to the entrance of the Harbor.

Flaco climbed up onto the fly bridge and took a seat next to Shorty, who was lost in his actions. "Hey, Chiquitico What are you doing?"

Shorty said nothing and pointed in the direction of the swimmer, who was now close enough to clearly see.

Flaco stood to take a look and then he sat down again. He turned to Shorty and said, "Now you look."

He pointed to the west, and the mouth of the harbor.

With a nervous twitch in his voice, he said, "You shouldn't get involved with this."

Shorty dragged his eyes away from the swimmer and saw the gray jet boat making an impossible speed to their direction. It had a gun turret on the bow and a Cuban flag streaming from the stern. It would surely beat the lobster boat to the desperate man in the ocean.

Shorty dropped his tensed up shoulders and breathed out one word. "S-s-shit."

But he continued on, believing he could be helpful. He had no reason to think otherwise, because American boats are quick to aid with search and rescue efforts.

The Cuban Coast Guard vessel easily cut him off and spun around to bear down on the swimmer.

Shorty had to idle down and resigned himself to watch.

He saw the sunlight bounce off of the stainless steel gaff hook.

The Cuban gun boat slowed down slightly as two guards in light blue uniforms plunged the vicious hook into the back of the panicking swimmer. The momentum helped them to haul the thrashing man onto the boat.

With a foot on his back, and the business end of an AK-47 to his head, he stayed flat on the deck, where the actions of the guards couldn't be seen by American eyes.

Shorty glared into the evil stare of the Cuban pilot, who then laughed as he ran the gray boat, back into the harbor.

Flaco wiped the sweat from his face with a wad of paper towels. Then he made the sign of the Cross on his chest. He looked at Shorty and shook his head. "Man, you're fuckin' crazy."

Everything seemed muffled and in slow motion to Shorty, who watched as the Cuban flag disappeared behind the old fort.

Shorty could almost feel the steel hook in the ribs of another man.

CHAPTER 6
ISSA THE CAR

Mario Senior clobbered his head as he straightened up under the hood of his '56 Chevy. He kicked the bubbled chrome bumper and let out a long string of forbidden words and inappropriate phrases, then rubbed fast and hard on the quick-growing knot, as though this really might numb the sharp pain.

His pretty little wife popped her head out of the small lush garden and scolded her husband. "Is this the kind of language to use around your young daughters?"

She swayed her open arm, like she was introducing her children to an adoring crowd. The two little girls, standing on a rickety card table to reach the clothes line, were absorbed with family chore time.

The father said, "Sorry, Mommy, I'm just having some words with our old friend Issa," which is the humorous name they had for the ancient car.

He turned the volume down on his mouth, but continued to whisper the cuss words, thinking they might fix the funny accident.

There was a sweet nature to their marriage; their personalities flowed easily together. She was easy to laugh in her wonderfully feminine way. He was always the unintended clown.

It was a challenge to keep the classic American cars running, but a privilege to have one.

They were the last remaining artifacts of a prosperous time gone bye. Trading parts, and sometimes even making them, were necessary skills. Too many people in Cuba had no wheels at all and had to pay for a bus or taxi. Bicycles and walking were popular modes of getting somewhere. But actually having a car was something special.

Money did exist, but it was rare, and hard to come by. One time Mario had a hand full of Cuban coins to add to his coin collection. The coinage of different denominations was made from cheap metal alloys that were so lightweight he could blow them out of his hand. It felt useless in the pocket.

೧೮೩೦

Only two decades before, this island country had been a thriving tropical playground for the United States. Fine hotels and restaurants lined the streets of every large city and town. World-class golf courses and high-end entertainment from places like Las Vegas could be found everywhere. Especially in Havana.

The duty-free rum and spicy cuisine brought in the eager tourists and their American dollars, providing for a fertile economy.

But the best resource of Cuba was the Cuban people themselves. Descended from many parts of the world, and with every face color, they blended into a singular culture.

Their art is made with fun, happy colors. When they speak, it's usually with passion and animated hand movements. In the warm tropical air they seem to walk to the throbbing rhythm of their classic island music.

Riding the popular wave of anti-corruption, Fidel Castro took absolute power over the country. It was then that the colors of life faded into the black and white of an old worn-out movie.

The vintage Catholic churches were the first to be closed. The stained glass windows and great arched doorways were boarded up and were now grown over with moss and vines. There was no room in a communist structure for people to believe they had a soul. They had the government, and they had Castro.

Then he seized all of the foreign and domestic interests. Everything had been made the property of the State. But it was when he put the knife of nuclear warheads to the neck of the United

States that the world no longer saw him as a Freedom Fighter. In his arrogance, he embraced the image of a loose cannon, and he thrived on this dangerous power. His political policies smacked of Communism and he became a torment to the United States, less than a hundred miles away.

But when the Soviet Union backed down during the Cuban missile crisis, he wound up losing the most dangerous game ever played. In retaliation for his aggression, the United States started an embargo that strangles the country Castro's narcissistic actions had cut the pulse of any possible emergence into the modern, free world.

Twenty years later, his country suffered an economic collapse. Cuba was no longer of strategic importance to its big brother Russians and has become a big money drain and a liability.

While his people suffered the ill reputation of being among the poorest in the hemisphere, the dictator remained one of the wealthiest men on the planet. Most of his money came either from the backs of his people or the illegal drug trade that found safe harbor in his waters.

The Dictator was frustratingly smart. He had a very real talent for controlling the masses.

He took good care of twenty percent of the population, and in return, they kept their eyes, and ears turned towards the rest.

They were a favored class, whose children enjoyed higher education, over the forced conscription in the military. These people were trusted, and devout loyalists to the government. They drove the newer, Russian-made cars and lived in the better housing.

Even quiet conversations of dissatisfaction could be overheard. Punishment was always severe and quick. Animosity and distrust grew between families and neighbors. One by one, people disappeared for ten year periods of time. Many of these so-called dissidents never survived the dark and dangerous prison system. For the more blatant offenses, or complaints made out loud and in public, there was a wall in every town that advertised fear. Bullet craters dug deep into the layers of paint and graffiti.

National Pride had been replaced by National Paranoia.

How long could this last, with the always thinking and always hungry human? It was raw instinct for people to feed themselves today, and try to gain enough to fend off tomorrow's starvation. Without freedom, the spirit was either beaten down to nothingness or some, perhaps the few, with a certain courage, would become angry and discontent. Eventually, these few either found a way to leave or became the seeds for another revolution.

CRED

The father opened a small white envelope of powdered aspirin and drank it down with the warm remnants of a flat beer. As he shook off his pounding headache, he resumed the search for a wrench around the cluttered yard. He finally found the rusted size he needed. He return to the clunker, mumbling a quiet grumble of aggravation with his repair.

It was only a week after his birthday when Young Mario threw his old leather suitcase into the back of a shiny brown Army truck.

The hundred mile ride up the coast took him farther from home than he had ever been. He had been sent to a military school that served as a boot camp for the draftees. The school shared a complex with the Cuban Coast Guard. It was stationed beside the old Spanish fort that overlooked Mariel Harbor.

Every day the two young sisters asked when their big brother would come home. The random letter or phone call came only once a week. It was a torturous wait for the close little family.

The parents knew that many of the new recruits were being trained to fight in one of the African wars.

Castro kept a potent military for the size of his country. It was rare for any of the conscripted young men to feel pride in serving their country, knowing that they might wind up becoming a soldier for hire. They could only aspire to be pieces in a global chess game.

Many would never return home. They were either killed in the jungle fighting somewhere far from home, or risk finding political asylum in the Free World.

CRED

The loud, raspy voice of an older lady carried over the line of junk that created the fence between houses. It was the fearful and badly abused wife of the dock master Warappo. He was also the government stooge in the neighborhood. He took great delight in the power he held over others. His polluted heart enjoyed the fear he held in his hand, and he thrived on the hatred he created. He was quick to trump up charges for anyone who crossed him.

"Oje-Oje me…Mario telephono. Dalle, rapidio." Quickly now, before my bastard husband comes home for lunch.

The family dropped the yard work and ran to the side window of the neighbor's house. She fished the long, coiled cord and receiver to their anxious hands.

Mario Senior held the phone out so they could all hear. "Speak loud, Mario, so we can all hear you."

Young Mario's voice gave a tear to his mother and joy to his sisters. His father's chest swelled with a proud breath, and he exhaled, leaving a slight taste of worry.

The son usually waited for his family to settle on the other end of the phone. Then he would spout off a fresh new joke. For everyone it was the best part of the week. He always made himself sound upbeat and confident. He wanted them to feel that his estrangement was only temporary. But on this day his bright, positive tone seemed to be a little forced. Even his joke for the week didn't seem to have the same timing, and effect, that his talent for comedy, would usually show.

Mario Senior began to feel flushed around his neck and his forehead went cool under the beads of his sweat. It was a father's intuition that grew quickly into the nauseous feeling that something was different, something was wrong, in the voice of his son. It came to him, that Young Mario was being listened to and closely watched.

The parents had heard about the flotilla of American boats. They quietly worried about the temptations that must be passing under the eyes of their free-spirited son.

Young Mario didn't mention anything about it, and the parents knew better than to expose their knowledge of it.

ଓଞ୍ଚ

Castro knew, that if he controlled information, he could control the people. The airwaves were dominated by government-censored propaganda. It was always a stream of misinformation, that was flavored with fear.

But real news in Cuba somehow managed to travel as fast as the fictional version, approved by those who had power. There was a quiet but immense grapevine that grew over and through the country. Its efficiency was powered by the hunger for truth.

The official reports had painted the recent events as a few troublesome Americans. Their efforts to persuade anyone to leave their beloved homeland would be fruitless. Anyone who dared attempt to leave would be marked as dissidents and punished accordingly.

But when tens of thousands of hungry and disillusioned Cubans storm the Peruvian Embassy, they were given asylum. A massive exodus was set in motion and became one of the biggest in world history.

The eyes of the international community, were once again focused on the almost-forgotten little country.

In the face of this growing embarrassment, Castro managed to turn the fast-moving events, to his favor. He knew there would always be some who could only be a challenge to his plan for a perfect society. These types either wanted him dead or wanted to leave. So he simply let them go. They would loosen themselves from the rest of the population. He would no longer need to worry about them, or have to deal with them the hard way. He saw opportunity in the American boats that swarmed into the harbor, eager to remove what he called scoria—scum—from his country.

He was also clever enough to use the Mariel Boat lift to empty his prisons and mental institutions. He sprinkled a few of his worst problems on each of the boats. They hid among the masses of the desirable people and would eventually wind up on the doorstep of the United States. This would create an unprecedented wave of crime that would give a historical black eye to the otherwise compassionate humanitarian event.

The vast majority of Marieletos who dared life for freedom would have to bear the reputation of this trickery after stepping on to the shores of freedom.

CRO

Excitement from the phone call lingered in the cozy home as the family settled in for the evening. The daughters were tucked in, and reading to each other before lights out. Mario Senior adjusted the rabbit ears on the old black and white TV set. Then he joined his sleepy-eyed wife on the freshly reupholstered love seat.

Few channels had clear enough reception to tune in and enjoy. Sometimes they would show a few old European or Russian movies. They considered it extra fun to watch the lips move different to the dubbed in Spanish.

All of the channels were heavily scheduled with State-created propaganda. The current events were distorted to convince the people that the rest of the world was a far worse place to be. Often times it was used to reinforce the fear.

Softly taking his arm from around his dozing wife, the father sat forward to better see the News Bulletin.

It appeared to be a uniformed young soldier who was bound and slumped over in a chair. As Mario Senior began to recognize the courtyard inside the old fort, his stomach burned and sent waves of prickly pain to his fingertips.

A single, low-key voice announced this young man is a traitor, and enemy of the state.

Six guards snapped to attention and raised their rifles to a firing position.

The shots sounded as one loud crack, jolting the mother from her sleep. Her eyes opened just as the young man, and his chair, flew backwards in pieces.

The father jumped up and then knelt between his wife and the TV screen. He held her waking face with his hands, until his eyes gained control of hers. With a forced calm, he told her; "That was not our son. That was not our Mario It's OK, it's OK."

Without a sound, she ran to the room with their children and jumped onto the bed. She pulled her sleepy daughters under her protective embrace. Her fierce gaze bounced from door to window. Any danger would have to face a Mother Lion.

Mario Senior stared insecurely at the screen and twiddled his thumbs. His brain raced, and a few of the words found their way to his mouth. In a firm, convincing way, he spoke out loud, to himself. "This was not our son. That young man was way too thin to be Mario. Please God, tell me that was not my son."

CHAPTER 7
THE HARBOR

Ten days had passed since they entered the harbor, and there had been no word about the eleven people they had requested to bring back to the United States.

A fog of rumors circulated throughout the three thousand American boats that were now trapped in Mariel Harbor. It was a shaky source of information and no one was clear about their situation.

The day before there had been a confusing opportunity for anyone who wanted to leave, to do so then, before Cuban authorities sealed off the harbor. Those who remained would have to stay and accept the bumbling management of what was growing into an unprecedented exodus.

Given that choice and all the uncertainties, Shorty was ready to pull the mud anchor and bring the boat home, even in the face of protests from his passengers. He believed that he had stayed long enough to have earned the money they paid, whether they retrieved their loved ones or not.

But when the older woman, Esperanza, quietly wrung her wrists, and wept, Shorty allowed himself to get lost in those painful eyes. He knew that if he left now, she would be losing her family once again. It was in that moment when he realized this event was an emotional investment that went way beyond any money.

It was a hard decision to make without being able to consult with Dagger, who would be expecting his boat to return by now. But Shorty chooses to tough it out and stay, even with all of the guarantees for regret.

Overnight two Russian gunboats stationed themselves bow to bow across the mouth of Mariel harbor. From this point on, no one else could enter, and only the government processed boats could leave. The promise of returning with chosen people seemed to weaken for the Americans in the harbor. They watched the overly loaded boats that could leave, and saw the reality of what was to come.

⊰⊱

Each day felt longer than the one before, and the boat became smaller and smaller to a man who was allergic to confinement. It was too hot, and way too sticky, to be so early in the morning.

Shorty pulled himself up to the cabin roof where he sat to sip his coffee. It was too sweet, and only half warm. But it was a small comfort that reminded him of home.

This was his usual spot, until the sun rose high enough to drive him down below, and into the shade with his passengers.

On a dried and wrinkled page of a spiral notebook, he scribbled another few lines of original song lyrics that always seem to come from out of thin air.. They were sad and full of self-pity. He decided they wouldn't be worth any accompanying music. But just spilling the thoughts out of his head and onto the paper seemed to cool his burning claustrophobia.

More than anything, Shorty wished that he had brought his guitar.

He never brought his guitar on the boat, no matter how much he wanted it with him. He believed the salt air might do damage to the instrument. It had served him well when he was a kid and played in a few country rock bands and now it was his best possession.

Shorty was a closet song writer. Only a few of his closest friends or family knew this about him. His music was a personal kind of hobby. It would be hard to find a private place on the boat, where he could immerse himself without being observed. With all of this time to waste, he could have, at least been practicing his scales.

When he grew tired of writing, he leaned back against the windshield and closed his eyes and tried not to acknowledge the pokes and jabs of waiting. Patience was one quality that the young man could never pull off. As far as he was concerned, patience was a virtue for somebody else to have. He would rather punch a wall than wait around for anything.

Usually, Shorty enjoyed his own good imagination. But with too much time to pass, it became like an enemy. He made himself sick with belligerent worries doing battle in his head.

He imagined Kim Sue in a hundred different scenarios of infidelity. He also dreamed up a thousand excuses to beat the crap out of the obnoxious Flaco.

Not long after lunch, his gut grinding would make him crave a soothing new habit. He never cared much for hard liquor before. But with a big help from Flaco, the beer was finished. The cheap Cuban rum had started to taste pretty good, even with just a splash of Cola for sweetness and color. Some days the alcohol calmed the brain, and numbed his stomach. On others it inflamed both. Either way, it made some of the time disappear from his short term memory. He chugged the liquid time-killer in a way that almost knocked him out. As though, he would wake up from a good hard drunk, and the present would, somehow, magically become the distant past.

He looked down into the thick, brown-gray water with toilet paper and trash slowly floated by. He shook his head and thought about the pristine natural lagoon that he saw on the first day, when it had been clear enough to see the bottom.

Shorty climbed further up into the fly bridge and stood on the bench. This gave him the best elevation for his curious eyes to scan the Harbor. He did this for hours every day.

Three thousand of every type of vessel was corralled into the sheltered water. He began to realize that he was having a lesson on civilization, and how it tends to follow the gathering of people.

From early on, as the harbor filled, different styles of boats would shift and move around, until they segregated themselves into little neighborhoods. He watched a whole new town emerge. Instead of houses, there was boats, and instead of streets, there was water.

The shrimp trawlers and larger vessels favored the deeper water in the middle. Some tied off side by side and shared one anchor. To the young man, they looked like duplexes and row houses, and they seemed to give community to a similar ilk of people.

The sport fishing boats and high-end yachts seemed to like northeast corner, closest to the hastily erected Government Center.

On the land were several big, green canvas tents. One had a Red Crescent on the side. They sat close to a set of long narrow docks that penetrated into the water, marked by an oversized Cuban flag that drooped, above the confusion of this staging area.

Shorty was on anchor with a small group of commercial fishing boats from his fish house. They were camped in the northwest corner, inside of the harbor mouth, just in case they needed to scoot out in a hurry.

Some of the American vessels had the foresight to bring skiffs and runabouts in tow. The smaller, more agile watercraft had been put to immediate use transporting people and goods throughout the Harbor.

The local Cubans who lived close by, brought in competition by converting their boats into water taxis and floating store fronts. Commerce was born and thrived in the once sleeping harbor.

American money and trade quickly became the life's blood of the Flotilla. The massive group of boats became one living and breathing environment of its own.

Thousands of conversations blended into a low-key, steady hum. It sparked with the squawk of radio chatter and passionate pangs of debate. The human music was constant, and an annoyance to Shorty, who preferred the quiet melody of the open sea.

Today during his usual look around, he didn't notice the vast flock of big black birds that were always circling in the distance. They appeared to spin around something hidden behind the staging area. He assumed there must be some sort of landfill or garbage dump that would attract such a vortex of vultures. But today they were gone.

Just as he lowered his binoculars and began to wonder what happened to the birds, a cold whip of wind parted his longish hair from behind. All of his senses tensed into one focus as he glanced over to the ocean side, where any foul weather would usually come from.

It was only calm blue skies, with feathery sails of clouds.

Then he turned to the southern side and looked at the sky over the land. He sat up with a sense of urgency when he saw a strange, haze-like halo rolling over the mountain and down towards the harbor.

He could smell the storm before it could be seen. He quickly swung down into the open cabin and took command of the relaxing passengers.

"Store everything that's loose down here in the bunk area," he said brusquely.

Flaco laughed. The others looked confused by the intensity in the young man.

There was no time to meet with the automatic challenge that always seemed to come from the thin man. Shorty just pushed him out of his way and cranked up the boat. The other passengers looked fearfully at his spontaneous actions, but quickly followed his orders.

He pulled in the anchor and yanked the excess rope over the gunwale. Then he told the ladies to go down below and put on the life jackets.

When he saw that everything on the deck was secured, he asked the two men to join the ladies in the water-tight lower cabin. He asked that they toss one of the life jackets up. Then he told them to wrap everyone in the cushions from the bunks and stay put until he tells them it's clear. They still weren't quite sure what was happening.

As they looked up to Shorty for an answer, a powerful gust of hot, heavy wind lifted the side of the boat, then quickly slammed it back down again.

He held on and said nothing as he closed the hatch behind them.

Shorty keyed his mike to connect with his brothers, who were aggressively in the same mode. The seasoned fishermen were mobile and in charge of their boats, as the voice of the harbor went quiet. They knew this would be rare weather. The best place to be was offshore on the leeward side of land. It would offer them the most room to maneuver and the best chance to stay in the face of the gale.

But the Russian gun boats refused their attempt to leave the harbor for the safer water.

Yogie was mad as hell as he turned his big boat around. He ran hooked up without regard for his wake. He zigzagged through the anchored boats and back into the cove.

He motioned to Shorty and another captain to follow. He re-anchored in a small open area, and left a long scope on the rope. Facing the south, and the oncoming Super Storm, he backed his boat down until it set fast.

Shorty did the same on the port side, as did the other captain on the starboard. All three settled on their anchors and they pulled their boats together side by side. They placed as many bumpers and tires between the hulls as they had, then lashed the boats close and tight together.

Yogie stood at the wheel in his cabin and told the two younger men to stay on their radios and try to do what he did.

The three became like one, with their anchors stretched before them and three motors to propel them in sync. The fishermen flexed and then braced to be overrun by the invincible force of nature.

The rest of the Harbor was just now taking notice of the deep blue and black wall that were rising from behind the mountains. It throbbed and bellowed with thunder and flashed the explosions of a thousand balls of lightning. At the base of the blackness was a gray-white spin of wind that looked like the mouth of an evil giant. A wall of hail rolled over the southern edge of the harbor. As the first assault plowed into the boats, an uproar of distant human screams followed it across.

The three crawfish boats throttled into the blast together. The icy beads slammed into the Plexiglass windows, which bent inward from the impact. They held up well, but it was a drastic hit for the boats that had regular glass.

As the wind let up in the front, it instantly reversed and fired the hail up into the cabin, peppering the fishermen from behind. They buried their necks and kept their faces forward as they were spun around and over their anchor ropes.

They were pushed a short way until the hooks reset. This left their sterns facing south and in the face of the next charge from the freak hurricane.

The three men wheeled back into the wind once again.

Several boats blew past them and were unable to make way. They went quickly out of sight, but could be heard as they crunched into the rock jetty that was not far behind them.

Now the black rain spilled over the mountain and grew to avalanche into the harbor. Everything collapsed under the wave of wind and water and disappeared into the belly of the circulating super storm.

Submerged in the rain, and with zero visibility, Shorty could barely see the outline of a massive hulk bearing down on them.

He signaled to Yogie and the other captain to the quick oncoming of a pile up. They ruddered to the port side and ran the motors full throttle. They managed to move over, just a few feet of being in the way.

It was two steel-hulled shrimp trawlers that had been tied off side by side, and slipped the foolishly planned single anchor.

The unstoppable barge slid sideways and, unfettered across the water, gathered some of the smaller boats in its path. A few were pulled under, while others slammed along the sides, unable to cut themselves free.

The tangled mass of wreckage passed close on Shorty's side. One of the outlying boats that were being dragged to their doom hit the side of his boat. It slid against his hull to the stern and in the second before it cleared one of the outriggers from a shrimper slammed the roof of his cabin. Then it snagged on the winch just behind his captain's seat.

The crawfish boats were now being dragged with the massive wreckage. Shorty was wild with the battle, but he found the clarity to grab a set of bolt cutters.

He slid down his deck, and began popping the cables that gripped his boat. The heavy block and tackle, and its brace, finally broke away from the fiberglass hull.

Before it tumbled over the stern and set the three boats safely loose, one of the half-inch cables snapped and gave a savage whip across his shoulder.

It cut a good gash, and the impact slammed Shorty face down on the deck. But like a big cat, he sprang back to his feet and never once put his hand to his wound.

He balled his fists, walked into the wind, and fought his way back to the wheel.

He looked over to Yogie, who was watching closely, and gave him a crazy laugh.

Yogie made a half a smile, and raised his wet, bushy eyebrows, and yelled, "Son! Are you gonna live?"

Shorty looked at his shoulder and screamed, "Hell, I got to live, They ain't gonna let me in Heaven."

The great storm lasted for an unremembered number of minutes. Everyone who was in Mariel Harbor on that day thought it was the end of the world.

೦೩೮೦

A strange quiet settled into the soupy fog that covered the basin. One side of the sky was beginning to lighten and gave the promise that it was over. As the air cleared, the shapes of boats, broken and whole, came into sight. Moaning and sharp pangs of pain rose from the remnants of the terrible battle between the flotilla and the great storm.

When Shorty opened the hatch, Esperanza flew out and wrapped her arms around him. She sobbed with relief.

Eduardo put a firm grip on the young man's forearm and thanked him repeatedly. His wife quickly set about tending the cut on his shoulder.

Flaco came out last and couldn't make eye contact with Shorty. He folded his arms and walked to the stern. Then he took a sober look from the epicenter of this holocaust.

The passengers and mates from the three boats were now out on the decks. One by one they began to speak with each other. But only in a solemn whisper or a thankful voice, to God. Slowly, their eyes opened to the panorama of destruction that stretched as far as anyone could see.

Shorty was humbled and thought that if he tried to speak, nothing would come out. He remained quiet, and worked with the other crew mates to untwist the three anchor ropes.

The shifting, circling wind had been clocked at ninety miles per hour. Now, it was gone, leaving a breath of warm, close air.

He bit down on his teeth, which were still trying to chatter from his residual fear. A feeling of peace, and contentment, was trying to enter into him. He did his best to ignore the hot pain that was beginning to catch up to his injury.

The young man started to untie his boat from the others so he could once again be mobile. He felt the need to navigate through the mess and take a look around. Perhaps he could be of help to some of the others who didn't fare so well.

Survivors, began to appear everywhere around then. Some were clinging onto the shards of boats, and a few were in the water hanging on the anchor ropes of those that were still intact. At least two bodies floated face-down and were close enough to the crawfish boats to be seen.

Everyone, without a question, would dig into the monumental, recovery of the still-living flotilla.

Yogie was chewing on a sandwich and drinking a beer like nothing ever happened. He walked over to Shorty and handed him a cold one and helped with the lashings.

"Hey, Chiquitico, how's your arm?"

"Ah, no biggie. The cut ain't so bad, but my damn shoulder feels like it's broke." Then he pulled up his shirt sleeve to show the purple bruise that was spreading from his shoulder, to his collar bone.

Yogie winced. "Damn, boy. Oh, well, you gotta be tough to be dumb."

It was one of those funny lines that Dagger would always use to describe the sometimes clumsy Yankee. They both took a big laugh and it served them well.

Then Yogie nodded over to the thin man, who was standing at the stern and looking the other way. He lowered his voice and asked Shorty; "How good do you know that prick over there?"

"I know him well enough to know that he's pissin' me off."

Yogie goes on to say; "I've seen him around the docks for a while now. He's looking for a couple of boats to go do the Razzamatazz."

Everyone around the docks knew that word very well. The crawfish boats were built for speed, and to carry a heavy load in shallow water or open sea. They brought a top dollar value to the drug smuggling trade. A boat like the one Shorty worked on would bring the owner enough cash for a healthy retirement. If it got busted, it would become confiscated and the owner would just claim it was stolen. If it managed to make it through, it would be used to bring in several more loads of pot and cocaine.

Eventually it would be scuttled, to make the evidence of a dirty fortune disappear.

Yogie whispered, "I bet he's been workin' on Dagger to get this boat."

Shorty flashed his eyes to the back of the thin man.

"You need to keep an eye on him," Yogie continued. "That's the kind that will try to off ya if you get in his way."

Shorty thanked the captain for the heads up. Then he dove back into his thoughts, which centered on a new fear. Now, Flaco's bad attitude towards him was beginning to make some sense. At least he finally understood the motive and what to look out for.

But just the thought that Dagger would even consider selling the boat out from under him felt like a knife blade in his chest. For several years, he had gone above and way beyond to prove his worth. He truly believed he was the next in line to become captain of this boat, one that he loved so much. It was his only real plan for the future.

Further thinking made him realize that the thin man wouldn't have to try so hard to discourage him, if Dagger wasn't so reluctant to cash out his boat.

CHAPTER 8
THE LONG BREATH

Over many long centuries, the ancient walls of the old stone fort endured a thousand attacks from nature and from man. Only a few scratches marred the gray patina of the rock.

The rock walls were the only thing in that part of the world that did not acknowledge any pain from the great storm.

The military school and Coast Guard complex were housed in newer buildings, next to the old fort. Much of the sheet metal roofing was ripped and hung from a few loosened nails. Most of the windows were victimized by flying shards of debris. Shattered glass was like razor blades stuck in the thick carpet of grass in the yard.

Minutes before the gale hit, the young recruits had been filed into the stone-walled chapel and were contained there for the duration of the weather.

After it passed, they were issued knee-high boots and heavy leather gloves to begin the work of cleaning up. They were led around the base of the old fort and down the path to the jetty. The orders were to search for survivors and bodies in the water and on the rocks around the Facility.

Young Mario wasn't the only one whose head was swimming with the temptation of escape. After all, thousands of American boats within a few hundred yards. And now, with all the fresh confusion, provided by the great storm, the young recruits could not be trusted by the higher-ups. There was no lapse of being relentlessly observed.

Ten days earlier, the desperate attempt to escape by the swimmer had brought harsh scrutiny down on the young draftees. They had been mustered together and forced to bear witness to the public execution.

The shocking loss was still fresh in the mind and caustic to the heart of Young Mario. The swimmer was from his home village of Los Villos. They had known each other's faces, but became closer during their training together. They secretly spoke of desertion, but the swimmer ignored the wisdom of Young Mario and couldn't wait for the perfect moment.

From the first day of his conscription, Young Mario felt the bite of discipline. It seemed like his spirit was forced to follow behind him, wearing handcuffs. Every day, his mind went out to sea while his body served out the sentence he never deserved.

Every night, he planned every possible plan to set his wild energy, free. For him, there was no choice. He had to escape the doom that waited for him in Angola.

Young Mario put on the look of doing his job. On the inside, the burn became stronger, as the chance to escape came closer.

Hammers and saws were beginning to make the sound of recovery around the harbor. There was the shrill whine of hundreds of boat motors backing down and pulling ahead to re-anchor. The outgoing tide jammed miles of debris against the shoreline. It slowly swirled into a pileup on the rocks just inside of the Jetty.

Through the buzzing of work came the heavy breathing of the survivors. There was fearful yelling, nervous laughter, and sobbing, tones of hurt and regret.

The Sun was once again hot, burning down hard on the disabled boom town of boats.

Vermillion red shone on the arms and legs of the lucky Americans who lost their boats but found the barnacle-covered rocks and pilings to hang onto.

Young Mario's squad, was agile on the wet, slippery boulders as they helped the stranded, to the safety of land. He was quick to enter the water when it was needed.

There was only one officer with the squad, and he was armed. He coordinated the rescue attempts and made frequent head counts on the draftees.

The desire to escape, made Young Mario feel lightweight and made his legs shake. He tried to look exuberant in his work, as he waited for the perfect chance.

Throughout the afternoon, his squad had pulled eleven suffering people from the rocks. They administered as much triage as they knew. One corpse was recovered from the cabin of a partially sunken boat drifting with the debris. She was a young American girl with long blond hair and the smoky eyes of fresh death.

Young Mario was the one who pulled her out, and with tears he gently placed her on the grass in the shadow of the old fort. The recruits were deeply affected. Some wept, while others looked away. He tried to see her as she had been a few hours before. As a happy, pretty girl, painted with life. His heart ached for the family that would have to identify their loved one.

The officer snapped a picture and filled out the location on a tag. With a matter-of-fact attitude, he looked at his watch and led his squad around the corner of the wall, towards the inlet.

Young Mario saw the seconds that he needed to make himself disappear from the invasive eyes of the government. He looked up to the guards on the bell tower and saw that they were focused towards the ocean side.

When the last recruit turned the corner, he filled his lungs. Then he let half of the air out as he slipped into the murky water and under the thick mat of debris that clanged along the jetty.

Almost immediately he wanted to turn around. But with the first long breath he made a strong kick and found the bottom.

Now he had committed treason and there was no turning back. He prayed that the water would remain his friend.

In the summers back at home, Young Mario always entered the much celebrated deep diving contests. Age groups from small boys to old men would compete at free diving. With only their lungs, they dove to depths of more than sixty feet and stayed down for minutes upon minutes. Those who went the deepest and stayed down the longest won prizes and became local celebrities.

Since he was a toddler, Young Mario had either won or placed in the traditional games. He became a crowd favorite by staying under so long that the spectators became worried. Then he would slowly appear from the depths, holding a sizable grouper by the gills, just for the added excitement.

Today, it was no game. He would have to become one with the water to continue with his life.

Vibrating with adrenalin, he swam like a dolphin across the silty bottom. Always with one hand out to feel his way through the sunken debris. He slowly made way against the slight current until his chest hurt and his skin burned.

Halfway into his first assent, he hit a partially-submerged piece of boat. Fighting the powerful impulse to inhale, he lost his direction to the surface. He cleared his nose, and followed the bubbles up until he found the air.

He let only his face emerge from the water, suppressing the sound of his gasp. As he took in the new breath, it flushed his body and reawakened his senses.

He slowly raised his eyes and ears just above the water line, and hoped beyond all hope that the top of his head blended into the floating mass of trash. When he turned to see the land, he was hit with another pang of fear. He saw that he had only made a short distance into the harbor.

It appeared like there was a lot of movement at the base of the wall around the old fort. From the bastions he saw the scopes of rifles searching the water around him.

A loud siren rose from the school that signaled his escape. It quickly sent him back down under the cover of the depths. He managed to make his way to a large engine box bobbing with the storm debris. He carefully swam up inside, and found a small air pocket in one corner.

The mind of Young Mario flashed with danger. Would he be shot the next time his head rose above the water? If he was caught, he was sure that the swimmer's fate would also be his. Would his family ever know what happened to him?

He thought the hard thought, that these could be the last few minutes of his short Life.

His blood chilled from the water and the worry.

Young Mario had been immersed, for nearly an hour, and the early signs of hypothermia began to cripple him. Even warm tropical water is cooler that Human Blood.

Everything seemed to do battle with his strength. The air remaining under the engine box was losing its ability to quench his lungs. He had to leave the shelter that hid him from the hunting eyes.

He forced himself into a clear image of his goal. To find an American boat that would stow him away and smuggle him to freedom.

He slowly emerged from the floating engine cover.

The shadows of sunset draped across the harbor, with shades of night falling in behind them.

His eyes were on the water line as he felt around for anything to hide with. His hand found an empty black trash bag that floated flat on the surface. He ducked under and lifted the edge for his eyes to see.

Once again his hopes took a plunge when he saw that the closest American boats were still a distance away. He slowly turned and peered back at the looming old fort.

Now he could only see one guard on the wall, and the area where he entered the water seemed deserted. He couldn't be sure, but maybe his escape was overshadowed by so many other emergencies created by the great storm.

He was still hidden in plain sight, and the risk of losing at his desperate attempt was impossibly high.

Dusk had finely grown into night and it was high, slack tide. Boat lights were popping on in the Flotilla. They shined into the green water and illuminated the suspension of filth.

Dark patches, and large pieces of trash to hide with, were now becoming hard to find.

He made three more long swims along the bottom and deeper into the Harbor. Still using the trash bag for cover, he could now hear the conversations in English, both distant and close.

From the beginning, he had realized that he only had a half of a chance. It was only luck that could save him now. His body cramped, with every little motion, and his senses were far too numb to continue any further.

Young Mario had to choose a boat and plead for his life. He prayed that whoever was on board would aid with his escape and not wind up turning him in.

He brushed up against an anchor rope and tried to swim past it. But he had to hold on to it so that he wouldn't breath in the water. He hooked his arm over the sway in the rope and struggled to hang onto consciousness.

In the gray of his thinking, he tried to remember the words he chose to use in his last letter home. Knowing that all correspondence would be censored, he used a line that only his Father would be able to read into: I can't wait to take a ride with old Issa.

Issa was not just the name of their old American car. It was also the name of his mother's sister who lived in Key West. He hoped his family knew what he would try to do.

A wobbling beam of light settled onto the slits of his eyes. It made him see colorful moving shapes and dots. A splash against his neck made him clutch the anchor rope and try to pull himself up. He thought of the bull sharks that frequent the harbors and inlets at night.

Then the hard plastic of a life ring drifted against him. He heard a quiet woman's voice, in his own language tell him not to say a word and to hold on.

Hunched over the life ring, he was gently pulled to the stern and through the tuna door of a fine new sport fishing boat.

His eyes were almost swollen shut, but he could make out the shadows of a woman and man, who were wrapping him in warm, plush blankets.

Then he could feel himself being lifted and carried, then placed on a deep, soft cushion. His lips eagerly mouthed the sweet water with disbelief. He still wasn't quite sure if he was alive, or if he was entering into heaven.

Again he heard the soft voice of the woman. She whispered for his name.

He stretched open his eyes and slowly focused on the most beautiful face he had ever seen.

His coughing voice struggled. "It must be true."

She leaned closer. "What must be true, Mr. Young Man from the Water?"

He forced a painful smile and said, "My mother always said that there would be angels You must be one of those angels."

She smiled her pretty smile and put her hand against his cheek. Then she held a paper cup of water to his mouth. "Yes, Mr. Young Man from the Water, your mother is right. Someday we will all see the angels. But you, my friend, are not dead yet. My name is Rosa."

CHAPTER 9
CHICKEN-FRIED NAKED

Less than a week after the great storm, Shorty was ready to jump off the boat and dive for sea urchins. Not that there were any to be found.

Stir crazy was no longer the problem. He had reached that point, and beyond. From his many miles of pacing, there was a circle of shine on the deck. He was almost sick from the waiting that now seemed to have no end.

His passengers had managed a few day trips into Havana and returned freshly showered, with arm loads of food and novelties. They encouraged the frustrated young man to take a break from the harbor and see a little more of Cuba while he was here.

Until this morning, he had refused to separate himself from the responsibility of his boat.

He hailed one of the taxi boats and freed himself from the same forty five feet of fiberglass that had been like his prison for nearly three weeks. It felt strange, and gave him a little guilt, when he stepped away from his home in the harbor

The only way for the Americans to see a limited part of Cuba was through the staging area. Under the big, drooping flag was the government tents. It was the center of operations for everything concerning the boat lift.

Like a web, miles of wires hung from the temporary power poles and antennas of every configuration.

Everything was thrown together as it was needed for the random and continuing event. Nothing about the process seemed to be consistent other than the confusion, and also the menacing Vultures, who were ever circling beyond the ridge. He wondered how many more long weeks he might be held here against his will.

Shorty stepped onto the embarkation dock and into the commotion. When his feet first hit the land, his body swayed. After eighteen days on the boat, it was a welcome feeling.

His frustration began to subside now that he was actually in motion and going somewhere.

He politely ambled through the groups and lines for the tents and made his way to an area that seemed to be offering bus rides to Havana. As he waited to board, his eyes were pulled to an unmoving line of people that stretched over the ridge and under the circling scavenger birds. The line ended on one of the long docks that stretched into the harbor and stopped next to an empty American boat.

This was his first look at the refugees. Shorty appeared tough, but he had a gentle heart. What he saw troubled him very deeply. He had never seen people in such bad shape. Even from a distance he noticed how thin most of them were. Many were sitting on the dirt, and the few who were standing, seemed to sway in the heat. They seemed to make no noise other than painful groans and their eyes seemed large against the hungry faces.

Shorty couldn't believe that so many would be crammed onto that single boat.

Eventually Shorty boarded an old French-made bus with torn seats and no air conditioning. He smiled at the familiar sounds and accents of the Americans who shared the ride.

Finally relaxing, he leaned back in the seat and looked out under the crack in his window.

Once they entered the mainland, he was quite taken by the vintage American cars. It felt like he had entered a time machine. They seemed to be everywhere and would be Cream Puffs to any classic car collectors in the States. Shorty would have loved to own one. He imagined himself tooling around the streets of Key West in a 1950s Chevy. He would fit right in among the mopeds and bicycles on Duval street.

He also saw many Cuban people walking along the highway. It struck him that maybe most didn't own a car at all.

During the ninety minute ride to Havana, Shorty consumed every sight. Flocks of lime green Parrots. Pineapple plants as far as the eye could see. It was all new terrain for his interested mind to absorb. The soil looked rich and black, the kind that could grow anything. The tropical colors and smells made him feel like he was entering into a rich and beautiful oil painting.

The road they were on was paved, but broken, with potholes, and patches of fresh gravel and tar. It rocked the bus along the way.

As they entered the outskirts of Havana, he began to see a city in a deep decline. The historical architecture looked like it was unkempt for many years. In Shorty's mind, he felt bad for the waste, but saw potential in the ruins of such a cool place.

He thought that the only thing needed to start a Renaissance would be a little free enterprise. But he sensed the hopelessness emitting from the defeated-looking people.

What stood out the most to Shorty were the looks of fear and the lack of genuine smiles on the faces of the streets. He felt that there was once a powerful, energy in this Country. Now it seemed to be sleeping, and seemed to have little desire to wake up.

The bus stopped at a golf course that at one time might have been high end. The futuristic lines and faded pastel paint on the club house would have been fashionable in the 1950s. Now it looked drab and boring.

The grounds seemed like they were freshly mowed. But the greens and fairways were unraked and there was no golfers. It was obviously prepared in haste to try and make it look like it was still in use. A sorry attempt to impress the Americans.

When he stepped off the bus, he had a craving for something cool to drink. Something to loosen up the brain. Next to a sprawling Banyan tree, he saw a thatched hut that looked like an outdoor bar.

Shorty watched as a dark-skinned bartender put on a show with a machete and a green coconut. His bare foot held it on a stump, as he took one long chop, to cut off the top. It was a close miss, but he managed it, without spilling the milk, or cutting off his toes. Then he added a long shot of amber colored rum, and squeezed in half of a key lime.

Shorty thanked the personable mixologist for the unique presentation and overpaid for the drink. He tossed the paper umbrella and took a long sip. He enjoyed the shade for a little while.

Surprisingly, the Bartender spoke very good English. Shorty was flattered to answer his many questions about the United States.

After a few moments of becoming fast friends, the bartender looked around nervously, then pressed a tightly-folded piece of paper in Shorty's hand. He made a strong eye contact with the American and pleaded with him to request the names on his list. They were his close family, and he was trying every possibility to get them on a boat.

Shorty was taken aback by the hopeless request, and in a heartfelt way he said, "I'll try, but I'm not sure that I can."

Then the bartender gave him a firm handshake and his eyes begged.

The earth and grass felt wonderful to walk on. A loud buzzing came from a circular garden of flowers and weeds. It drew him near, but he never saw the first bee. He was overwhelmed and surrounded by hundreds of hummingbirds. Never having seen one before, he sat and watched the colorful birds, whose wings moved so fast they couldn't be seen. Shorty looked lost in his amazement.

Later he joined onto a line for a pay phone. It was still early enough in the day to have a little patience left for waiting.

The main reason for his trip away from the boat was to place two collect calls.

The first was to Kim Sue. But the phone rang and rang, with no answer. His jealousy rose up, as he wondered where she might be at this time of day. Once again his imagination was starting to hurt.

Then he nervously placed the second call to his captain. Someone picked up the phone, but said nothing. When the operator chimed in with, "A collect call from…"

Before the operator could finish, Shorty heard the hang up.

A new wave of worry flooded through the young man. He could feel the vibes of anger from Dagger run right through the phone line.

He hung up and walked away. Then he stopped on the sidewalk to close his eyes and turn his face to the sun.

The image of refugees he had seen earlier was hard for him to absorb but it made him feel righteous for still being in Cuba. Now more than ever he wanted to make this trip into a good thing. Giving a repressed people their freedom gave him a new cause.

When the big young man smelled food, he completely forgot about his painful future. His pace picked up and he almost ran to the restaurant.

As soon as he entered the double doors, he found himself in a building thick with blue flies.

He thought it was impossible to serve food this way and he almost turned around. But he saw that the cheap looking tables were full of Americans waving their arms, and trying to eat.

Shorty had been born hungry. His big frame was always in need of fuel, so he braved the dirty little dive bombers to place an order of fried chicken and soft yucca.

When he was served, he had to swat his way to the plate.

He never realized that chicken could be fried without any breading of some sort. It was a battle to eat the chicken fried naked before the terrible flies could deposit their eggs.

Finding it impossible to finish this meal, he left, feeling prickly, agitated, and with a hollow stomach.

He ambled over to join another line. It was for a bus that was going to the only other place the Americans could go. It supposedly offered Showers.

Down below, on the boat, he had managed to rig a private area for his passengers to use for a bathroom. It was easy enough to replenish his fresh water tanks at the staging area, even though it was not drinkable. So far, staying clean on the boat was inconvenient, but still possible.

But he did look forward to some hot water to scrub a few layers of the harbor from his skin.

It would give him a chance to see a little more of Cuba, and make his day away from the boat worthwhile. At least he was getting a little break from the boredom.

On the crowded bus he found himself trying to hide the smell emitting from his ugly orange fishing boots by pulling his pant legs over the tops. How embarrassing. In the confusion of leaving home, he had forgotten to bring a pair of real shoes.

Everyone who worked around the docks wore the white rubber boots, except for Shorty. His were a strange florescent orange color. They had been the only size thirteens on the shelf at the Marine Hardware Store.

In a way they sort of fit with his individualistic style.

But pulling lobster traps is a wet, sloppy job. His yellow rubber coveralls were always too short for his long legs and never came over the tops of the boots. Seawater would fill them and cause him to empty them often as he worked. The mixture of fish blood, bait and old rubber made for an unrecognizable smell. It also made for the perfect people repellant.

The bus turned onto a straight highway on a long stretch of seawall. He opened the window to better see the store fronts and hotels that made the Havana skyline. Many of the beautiful old Art Deco buildings seemed to be vacant and not open for business.

Then he stood up for a better look at the ocean with no beach. The water was deep blue, and seemed too deep to be so close to land.

There was a broad sidewalk with a short stone wall and a rail between the roadway and the breakers. An occasional wave would launch a fan of spray over the walkers and the lookers. Colorful people of every kind either strolled along the walkway or stood staring at the distant white hulls of the liberating boats that were heading out to sea.

The bus parked close behind two others in a circular drive, in front of a three-story hotel. The name on the marquee was The Triton. It appeared to be quite the resort, back in the day.

Shorty reluctantly stepped down into the river of Americans that flowed into the lobby. Crowds always felt restrictive to the young man who thrived in his own space. For him, it was like walking in water up to his neck. He contained his overage of energy and, with a painful smile, tried to avoid bumping into anyone or stepping on their heels.

To be standing a head above the rest, in a mob, did give him the advantage. He could navigate better and was able to see the whole interior of the hotel.

Classic photographs of the Rat Pack from Vegas, along with movie stars from the black and white days lined the rich burgundy wallpaper. Brass rails and velveteen ropes steered the wide lines to the window counters in the vast hallways.

An older, chunky Latina with a flirtatious smile handed Shorty a faded blue ticket torn from a large roll. He was able to squeeze close enough to grab it, as she flashed him her cleavage.

He gave her a hungry smile like she was the most beautiful woman on earth.

Then he looked shocked when he saw the number on the blue ticket was 863.

He turned to the crowd around him, and said, "I hope this isn't how many are in front of us."

So much for the hot water. But he was determined to wait for a real shower, even if it was a cold one.

Frustration burned his scalp during this period of slow motion. His feet and legs tingled, threatening to go to sleep on him.

Every step was only a few inches closer to the distant top floor and the lavatories.

By the time he reached the second landing in the stairwell, he realized he had to pee. *Shit!* He would have to start over in a different line to use a closer toilet. His only choice was to stay where he was. He squeezed his inner thighs against his parts, and it made him look pigeon toed. This was gonna take a while, so he tried to put his mind somewhere else.

On each level, there was a big set of windows that over looked the grounds behind the hotel. This gave Shorty some long moments to scan the gathering below for a familiar face.

It looked like a good outdoor party was developing in the grand courtyard and pool area. He noticed several booths that were serving paper plates, bending with the weight of black beans and rice. Each had a hand-pulled chunk of roast pork plopped on top. He had to sneak his shoulder to his mouth to catch the drool.

There was also a long bamboo bar selling mixed drinks in clear plastic cups to the loud and rambunctious Americans.

Like most young men, Shorty would let his eyes rest for a moment on every pretty lady in the crowd. But with Shorty, even just looking at other girls came with a little guilt. His old-school morality kept him from becoming too interested while he was in a committed relationship with Kim Sue.

But lately there had been more than just a few challenges to the trust he had in his little girlfriend. He was beginning to think that his proper behavior was a big waste of time. A voice in the back of his head told him, *Hell, what harm could it do? Just go ahead and look.*

He thought he had caught a glimpse of Eduardo in the corner next to the tennis courts. As far as he knew, none of his passengers had plans to leave the boat. So his eyes continued to search the area.

They rolled across the silhouette of a woman with long, wavy brown, hair. She was at some distance across the courtyard. His mind immediately switched from trying to locate one of his passengers to absorbing the perfect profile of this lady.

She held a drink and was having a lively conversation with several young men. They were captivated and had her surrounded. Her movements seemed to be delicate and with purpose. She was facing the other way and from behind he was held captive to her soft curves. He shook his head and whispered to himself, "Ahhh."

Then she turned her head to the side, and he could make out the symmetrical features and high intelligent forehead of a classic Latina beauty.

He shifted his weight from one leg to the other trying not to dribble any pee down his pant leg. But even with this powerful annoyance, he still couldn't keep his eyes off of her.

Suddenly she snapped her head in his direction and peered straight up and into the window where he stood. Her fiery eyes shot across the distance and she glared straight at the big gringo.

Shorty was frozen stupid. He couldn't move, he couldn't think, he didn't even have to pee anymore. *Busted!* he silently screamed to himself. Staring at someone's back side from more than a hundred yards away, and she caught him. And she didn't seem very happy about it, either.

Not sure what to do, he pointed to himself and mouthed the words, *Who, me?* He was still hoping she was looking at someone else, and not the Dunce that he felt like he was.

He wondered if this chick actually felt him looking at her, or what? For a few seconds she held Shorty in her gaze and jabbed him with an angry, violated vibe.

The Latina looked back to the men she was talking with and then slowly turned her head back his way. She rolled her big round eyes and gave him just the slightest pout of a smile. Then she politely left her conversation, and quickly walked out of his view.

He was left with a strange mix of embarrassment, and just a little urgency to finish this line and go look for her. Then he told himself that she was way out of his league anyway. Besides, he had a girlfriend back home. At least, he thought he did.

Just a sliver of soap and water colder than what he had back on the boat was all that Shorty would get from the two-hour line to the shower. But it was still invigorating, and felt almost civilized.

With his wet hair pulled back in a short tail, he entered into the afternoon light of the courtyard.

The crowd seemed to have thinned out enough for him to feel like he wanted to mingle. When he turned towards the bamboo bar, he ran head long into Felicia and Eduardo. Esperanza was close by, and they were all smiles. Even though it had only been a few hours, he embraced them like old friends and was truly surprised.

But he dropped his smile when he realized that Flaco must have been left alone with the boat. It made his guts grind a little to think about it.

The Fernandez couple openly disliked and avoided the arrogant thin man. Felicia confided that he made her skin crawl. Eduardo didn't like the way he tried to taunt his Captain Shorty.

Esperanza, in her mothering way, tried to keep the young man calm during tense moments with the problem on the boat.

Eduardo sounded reassuring when he said, "Don't worry, El Capitan There is nothing that Cucaracha could do with your beautiful boat." Then, with a big smile, he reached into his pocket and said,

"I've got the keys." He jingled them as he handed them over to Shorty.

The knot that had pulled tight in his stomach began to loosen as he said, "I guess it's better than leaving the boat with no one at all."

This was a friendly point he had to make, about their unplanned trip to land without telling him about it.

He decided to make the best, of the rest of the day. So he put his troubled feelings about Flaco away.

Food could always take over Shorty's undivided attention. While he was standing there talking, he finished two plates of the sloppy but deliciously spiced pork and black beans. It pleased his body with a relaxing energy.

When he finished, he gradually eased away from his group of friends and strolled through the Americans in the courtyard. He listened, trying to pick up any new information about the fix they were all in. Everyone seemed to have the same frustrations and confusion about the waiting time for going back home. It made him feel that at least he was not alone.

The image of the lovely Latina just wouldn't leave his mind. Even though it was only a hazy look from a distance, it seemed to have etched itself into his mind's eye. He scanned the faces as he walked, hoping to catch another glimpse of her. Not that he wouldn't fall back into a clumsy mode and look foolish all over again. He probably wouldn't find the courage to approach her anyway. Shorty had plenty of guts when it came to facing his dangerous work on the Ocean. His world of tough and testy men would rarely make him nervous. He was always comfortable with just about everyone. But a few times in his past, when he was standing before an extraordinarily good-looking woman, his knees would shake and the words would fall out of his mouth like cracker crumbs.

This particular little insecurity had left him looking like a fool before.

He really wanted to run into her again, but just the thought of it scared the crap out of the big tough guy.

Who was this girl? One who could embarrass him from a distance and without even a word? She must have thought he was just another dumbfounded goof who was staring at her.

But there was one thought that kept hammering at his brain.

Shorty was never real big on the mystical happenings of life. But he couldn't help but wonder. It seemed like she actually felt his eyes on her back side. In a crowd of many hundreds, she turned and shot her eyes right into his.

He thought it was strange, but maybe kind of cool, that there could be some unexplainable connection with her. He wasn't sure if it was a little smile that she gave him, but he clung to the belief that it was.

CHAPTER 10
THE DREGS

Eduardo insisted on paying for the water taxi for the ride back to the boat.

Shorty and his passengers had gathered on the bus ride back to the staging area. They shared a great deal of new information.

Apparently the politics back home had shifted. Three weeks earlier the American government had given its blessings to the Flotilla. But since it all began, more than a hundred thousand Cuban people were jammed through the tiny island city of Key West. There was only a two-lane road and long bridges that connected it to the mainland. Everything had come to a standstill, including the traffic all the way to Miami.

In order to try and stem the tide, the United States had begun to issue fines and confiscate the returning boats. The quality of processing such a flood of humanity was good but slow. The massive event was backing up and growing into a mess, with no end in sight.

Shorty had spoken to a number of Americans in Havana, which gave him a feel for how much longer his ordeal would last. It seemed like the turnaround time for entering the harbor and returning home was between three and four weeks.

He was advised not to confront or question any of the Cuban officials about their handling of the exodus. This might add more waiting time for those who, by now, were short on endurance.

Despite the many factors that were remaining. the progressive-thinking young man began to see a little light in the distance, one that would open up and illuminate the end of his quest. The possibility of putting this event behind him in a matter of days gave him the second wind that he needed.

As they neared the area of their anchorage, Shorty stepped up on the bow to direct the taxi boat. When they passed a few of the familiar neighboring boats, he began to feel the burn in his belly.

His passengers were also looking hard at the area and becoming worried. They should have seen the boat by now. When it became obvious that Flaco had moved the boat, they became vocally upset, and threw up their arms in anger.

Shorty pressed his lips tight and remained silent as he held back on his torrential rage.

As they idled over the exact spot where they left the boat anchored, everyone looked at the young man.

A few days before, Yogie had managed to find a flight out, via Venezuela, via Mexico, via Miami, to Key West. Shorty knew the antsy captain would not wait for too long. He left his big crawfish boat with his first mate, Pots and Pans.

Unusual nicknames were a part of the personality of the commercial fishing docks. Someone told Shorty that the wiry, funny guy got his nickname in Vietnam. Apparently he was a cook in the Army. But the troops decided his cooking was more dangerous than friendly fire, so they demoted him to dishwasher for the rest of his tour of duty. He still carried his name with pride.

Shorty had the water taxi pull a long side of Yogie's boat and he jumped on board. It looked deserted, but he knew that Pots was probably down below, snoozing. So he banged his fist on the hatch.

The young man never knew anybody who could sleep more than his friend. If this goofy man wasn't working or drinking, he was somewhere dozing off.

The guys made jokes about what he might really be doing with all of the time he spent down in the cabin.

Pots took his good own time waking up. He finally popped his shiny bald head out of the cabin and looked up at the stressed out young man. He opened his mouth wide in a loud, exaggerated yawn.

It seemed to turn around inside of him and exited as one big ripper of a fart. Then he grinned.

Shorty loved this Guy's humor, but he had lost all patience for anything. With a strained voice he said, "Hey, man, I need your help."

Pots stepped up on the deck with a meek look on his face and said, "Yeah, man, what's up? Dude, you look all kinds of pissed off."

When he saw the water taxi and Shorty's worried passengers, he looked over to where Dagger's boat was anchored.

Then he straightened up. Now that he was awake, he said, "What the fuck? Where's your damn boat?"

Without a second thought, he cranked up the motor on the crawfish boat and motioned Shorty's passengers on board. His own crew was off visiting somewhere in the Harbor.

He stopped Shorty's next words with the palm of his hand and with a fast, shaky voice, he said, "I get it. Let's go hunt that fucker down."

It gave Shorty a good jump of power to know he had a strong ally to help him recover the boat.

He knew that Flaco couldn't leave the Harbor with an empty vessel. It was pure audacity to take it upon himself to move Dagger's boat anywhere. It was the most brash challenge to Shorty's authority and responsibility that could be made. In Shorty's mind it would be the last.

The fly bridge on the bigger boat gave them a view of the whole harbor. It was slow going to weave in and out of the crowded flotilla and search for a boat.

Night was beginning to come on again, but soon enough Shorty spotted the outline of Dagger's boat. It was tied up quick to a frumpy-looking old shrimp boat.

Many of the shrimpers were family-run businesses and stayed within the boundaries of the law. The nature of work for the large, heavy-duty trawlers might keep them off shore, and away from port, sometimes for months.

But there were always a few dregs that would hide behind the business and involve themselves with dangerous and troubling activities. They were quick to hire a cold and cruel breed of men.

Like nomads they would cover great distances and switch home ports after each trip. For a man who was on the run, it was a perfect place to hide.

As they pulled alongside Dagger's boat, Shorty noticed that the motor was still running. For how long, and how much fuel was gone, he couldn't tell. There were also a few tools scattered around on the disassembled dash. Proof that the boat had been hot-wired.

It made Shorty cringe to see the boat tied off too close, without any bumpers between the hulls. It was grinding and slamming up against the side of the taller boat with every little wake that went by.

Pots put Shorty onto Dagger's boat alone and then backed down a few feet. He kept his eyes on a mean-faced fat man who glared down on them from the stern of the trawler. The black-vested biker with his beard that grew onto his chest called up to his cabin for Flaco.

As soon as Shorty set foot back on the boat, the helpless feeling of having his hands tied went away. It turned into a smooth and clear personal power.

Deep, loud voices sprinkled with sinister laughter moved to the back of the grimy shrimp boat.

Pots and Shorty's passengers could see the top of Flaco's Afro among his hard-ass friends.

Shorty immediately set about reattaching the wires and putting the dash back together. Then he inserted the key into its proper place.

When his passengers began to board, they each looked up at Flaco, who was wearing his tormenting smile. They showed their disdain for the arrogant thin man, but it was salted with a good bit of fear. They knew that this could easily become a hostile situation.

Flaco looked down at them, and gave off a seedy laugh as he held a bottle of rum. His jaws were grinding from cocaine.

He sneered, "Hey! How was your trip to Havana? Did you bring me anything? What? No little Cuban putas for Flaco? Well, dats OK. Esperanza will do just fine. Come on, Vejidica, climb up here and meet some of my compadres."

The ignorant comments to the elderly lady made Eduardo's face glow red and the veins popped out on his neck. He jumped back up on the gunwale and cussed Flaco in English and Spanish. Then he put his fist in the air and demanded an apology for Esperanza. Eduardo's fierce defense only triggered a loud, evil-sounding outburst of laughter from Flaco and his rough-looking entourage.

Then he raised his middle finger in frustration.

Felicia pulled her husband back onto the deck and hugged his neck from behind to restrain him.

Flaco's face went serious, and the laughter diminished into tension.

Pots stood by in the fly bridge of Yogie's boat with a cocky look for the shrimpers. He had his hand up between his legs, on a coach gun clamped under his seat. The double barrel, was ready if Shorty couldn't handle the evolving stand off on his own.

Back home the shrimpers and the crawfisherman were like two rival gangs. One on each end of the docks and oftentimes on each side of a bar or a club. The air between the two different types of commercial fishermen was usually charged with imminent violence.

Shorty knelt down on the deck and reached his long, sinewy arm up inside the wheel box. He felt around for a small lever, that opened a very well-hidden compartment. When he pulled his arm back out, his passenger's eyes went straight to the black nine millimeter in his hand. They were surprised, and frightened, to see this side of the gentle giant they had come to know. They flinched when he chambered a round. He checked the safety.

Esperanza held her hand out to him, and said, "No, Hijo."

Shorty turned to his extremely frightened passengers and said, "Look, you guys. You know me. I'm not inclined to let anything crazy happen. But I can't let that man back on this boat."

Then he grabbed his big cowhide knife and pushed it across a whetstone a few times. He examined the shiny edge against the rust of the blade.

The worry lines on his forehead funneled the sweat to his chin. It dripped on the floor. As he stepped one foot up on the gunwale, he turned and spoke to Eduardo.

"I'm gonna cut us loose. If anything happens, take this boat and haul ass back to where we were. Hang with Pots and make sure Dagger gets his boat back."

With the ladies whimpering behind him, he pulled himself around to the bow. Wearing the phoniest happy face he could muster, he chuckled and said, "Well, Flaco old buddy, old friend. Looks to me like you found a new boat to inhabit."

Flaco just glared at the big gringo. The shrimp trash behind him were beginning to look nervous.

It would have been easy enough to just lift the braided loop from the Samson post and cast off. But instead he looked away from Flaco and took two long swipes on the shrimper's rope. Then he looked straight at the thin man and touched the blade to the last strand. It popped and they drifted away from the trouble. He shook his head, spit in the water, and reclaimed Dagger's boat without incident.

CHAPTER 11
ROSA

In the early evening after the great storm, Rosa sat at a cushioned booth on the aft of the lightly damaged yacht, vanquished. Her eyes were closed but she wasn't sleeping. Silky fingers caressed the stem of a crystal wine glass that was half full with ginger ale. She was spending some hazy time in her most distant memories.

⊂⊃

A little girl with a blistered face was jolted out of unconsciousness. She felt the tearing crunch on the bottom of the open wooden boat when it drifted aground on Marathon Key. That little girl, Rosa, squinted painfully to open her salt-swollen and encrusted eyes. Blisters bubbled on her baby skin from a week under the relentless sun.

Her family lay in the bottom of the floating coffin, dehydrated and looking dead.

As a toddler, Rosa and her family had fled from Cuba during the pandemonium of Castro's takeover.

They had been against the brutal new politics that had infested their homeland. This made it dangerous for them to stay. They had had a successful life, but had been forced to leave all of their possessions behind. Their property had been confiscated and was now owned by the State.

Her father immediately found work in an American boatyard and over the years he muscled his way up and into the American Dream.

CRBO

Rosa's family now owned and operated a small but high-end boat building company in Jupiter, Florida.

When Rosa finished art school, she took over the design work for their business. She raised the demand even higher for the quality vessels that her family built. She appeared elegant and dainty, but few women held a 200-ton captain's license. She had been born to the ocean and could hold her own working around the boat-building docks.

The toughest part for Rosa and her family had been losing her older half-brother, who had been taken away and made to serve in the Revolutionary Army. His fate still haunted them, and the loss never softened with time. Deeply engaged in his work, Rosa's aging father would often slip and refer to other men with the name of his son, Catanno.

For years, her family had been paying ransom for dead-end leads on the bother's whereabouts. But in recent months they had found new reason to believe he was still alive.

One of her father's oldest friends, who still lived in Cuba, sent them a letter of hope. Catanno was indeed, still alive, and had long since shed his uniform. He managed to use the corruption of the government to obtain another name. But he chose to live quietly in the sparsely populated mountains, always afraid that he might still be recognized as a deserter from long ago.

Through a series of costly channels, they finally made contact with Catanno. The plan was made for him to make his way to Mariel Harbor and find his sister Rosa.

Each long day, she faithfully went to the staging area and suffered the lines to locate a brother she hadn't seen in twenty years. She only had an old photograph to go by. It was worn out from her trying to memorize his face.

It was an added difficulty to find someone who hid under an assumed name, especially under the nose of a suspicious government.

The empowered young lady was prepared to bribe, deceive and even use her disarming beauty to succeed with her mission.

She knew that her brother should have appeared by now, and she was fighting back against the looming disappointment. But even if she did fail, Rosa planned to rescue as many of her people as her boat would hold. She was determined to gift them with the same beautiful freedom that her family now knew.

Rosa's eyes opened and her memories disappeared behind the present, as her uncle sat down across from her. Tio Raul had a concerned look on his usually confident and comfortable face. They went into a quiet, secretive debate about what they should do with the young man from the water.

At first they had thought he was one of the storm survivors who had been swept from one of the nearby boats. But Tio Raul couldn't shake the feeling that he was an escapee from the nearby military facility. They both understood how things worked in Cuba. If they helped this young man and were caught, the government would confiscate the very expensive boat. They would also loose what was left of the possibility of finding her brother.

The decision weighed heavy on them both, because they knew that if the government had their hands on this escapee, he would face the ultimate punishment.

Rosa stood up and took a deep breath. She looked at her uncle with a fresh energy and asked, "What kind of tools did we bring?"

Together they applied their boat-building, skills and fashioned a safe place for the escapee to disappear into. The fumes of epoxy were strong throughout the early morning hours.

They cut the fiberglass under one of the crew's bunks and created a hatch with nearly invisible seams. A small vent fan was installed in a difficult-to-see corner. It was designed to enter on short notice, but would be too hot to stay in for any length of time. Outfitted with a few gallons of fresh water and some barbecued chips, it would do well on short notice.

No one could know, not even the people on the American boats who were anchored around them. The young man from the water would have to remain unseen, and always ready to quickly disappear into the newly made hiding place.

If the government eyes happened to look their way, it would be almost impossible to notice any evidence of a stowaway on board.

With the drapes closed over the windows of the state room, Young Mario would recover in a plush feather bed. For now, he would just have to lay back, and watch the color TV, in air conditioned abandonment.

CHAPTER 12
A SOFT KISS

Three angry-faced men aimed their hatred at the little Cuban girl when she opened the front door.

Mario Senior stood like a rock between his huddled, crying family and the men who hunted his son.

They were forced to watch the savage ransacking of everything that touched their life. Fear in the family and the rage of the father froze into silence against the breaking of glass and wood. All they owned now laid shattered around them.

The senior official stepped right up to the father's face. The father burned with the will of sacrifice when the government men finished and approached the innocence of his family. They would have to kill him before they touched his girls. The official dropped a paper from his fingertips. It floated from side to side down through the dust and settled onto the slashed carpet.

The hard-nosed men who had done all the damage were frustrated with being assigned this kind of duty. The more lucrative work was with graft and bribery back in the harbor. Wordless and mean, they stormed back out through the door.

Mario Senior pulled away from his wife's hardened arms and his daughter's trembling hands and ventured a look outside. On the sidewalk in front of the house, Waroppo stood with the proud look of importance. Then he hissed a smug laugh and walked away with a little out-of-character skip in his step. Mario turned back to his family, still huddled together amid the destruction. He spotted the paper the official had tossed onto the floor.

His hand shook so much that it was difficult for him to pick up the paper from the floor.

The face of his son filled most of the painful page.

Under the portrait was a barrage of deadly words to warn anyone who might help the fugitive. And in big print was the reward amount for the Loyalist who would turn him in, a reward spiced with privileges and additional food vouchers, not available to the common people.

Mario Senior had read and understood the hidden message that his son had used in his last letter.

At first he was angry with Young Mario to even consider such a risk. But he knew his son and there was no communication that he could use to sway any possible desperate choice. He suffered the week helplessly, knowing that Young Mario might try to make a break for freedom.

But the humbling rape of his house meant that they were still searching. It was good enough news for the father to know that his son was still alive.

The government's search would go on forever, and the mean-faced men would return. He knew the next encounter would be worse. It was no longer safe for the family to stay in Cuba.

Mario Senior and his wife had quietly considered a move to the free life for many years. They had family in the States, and the fishing was good. They knew that the fears they always lived with would never survive in the great country America. Always it was never the right time to try such a dangerous effort.

Now with Young Mario's attempt, and with the Straits of Florida full with boats, coming and going, Destiny had declared the timing for them.

As he gathered in the trembling of his stomach, The Father gave his eyes and soul to his sobbing wife and simply said, "Florida. Our son will see us in Florida."

For the following days, the family put on the air of repairing their home. In the quiet of the night, the plans were made for the dangerous escape. Their only choice was to cross the Gulf in the old family boat.

თ**ა**

For the eyes of Warropo and others who watched, the family openly behaved as if life went on as usual. Early morning saw the father walk down to the boat, like he had done since his childhood. As he passed the fish house and the evil little king, he was sure to smile and wave. But not too much of a smile could come from a man whose peaceful life had been recently violated. He was careful not to look too happy, or false in any way. This might awaken the suspicion that was always swimming in the rum-soaked mind of the dock master.

The smell of the Cuban coffee was wonderfully strong as it floated across the water and through the boats of his lifelong friends. They would join him one by one to sip the shots of sugary, thick drink. This would fuel the traditionally passionate gossip that working men in Cuba enjoyed during their down time. Waving their arms and closing face to face was a dramatic part of the language. Mario Senior sat on the gunwale with a simple smile and added little to the friendly noise.

What no one seemed to notice was the slight bulge under the father's shirt.

On every trip to the boat, he slipped a few more cans of food and soda into the tiny, cluttered cabin, and hid them under the fishing gear.

By lunch, he would return home. This was siesta time in small coastal towns like Los Villos. Generally too hot to accomplish any hard work, the village would fall into a sweaty and not very refreshing sleep. But it was a natural part of the routine in a life without a clock.

During the day, Warappo would rarely move from his seat in the shade of the fish house. No one could tell if his eyes were open, and watching, or if he was dozed off in a drunken funk.

At night the watch was taken over by the dock master's nephew. He was just as willing to turn in a friend or neighbor for the favor of the government. But he was much more alert. Together they were the constant eyes and ears of the Cuban government.

Few of the boats had been allowed to leave the basin since the

Boat Lift had begun nearly a month before. Most of the law enforcement and military was focused between Havana and Mariel Harbor. So far no one from the small fishing village had dared to try and escape the country.

To leave at night and become hidden with the darkness would be anticipated and watched for.

The family house sat up on blocks no different from most of the small homes in the Village. While pretending to make repairs, the father had to belly down into the tight, buggy crawlspace. He was looking for an armload of lumber to be seen with. He found a mossy green bottle against a beam covered with dirt. It was still corked and full, but had no label. As he held it up to a dusty ray of sunlight, he saw the chopped herbs settle to the bottom.

He remembered it was a gift from a visit, many years past.

Mario Senior had an aging uncle from the mountains who they called Jwajido, which translated to Hillbilly. The old man was proud to be the family nut job, but had long since passed away. They missed his funny visits and the strange gifts he brought from the mountains.

Knowing his uncle well, the father suspected the herb-infused rum was more than just flavored for taste. Many of the old-timers from the hills used medicinal plants that could be severely narcotic, and even hallucinatory. It scared the father so he had hidden it under the house where it remained, forgotten for years.

Finding the old green bottle provided the missing key to the plan for escape.

⊂঺ঌ

The next morning on his way to the boat, the father stopped at the fish house.

Already half drunk, Warappo slowly stood and wobbled into a jerking balance. He pointed at Mario Senior and snarled, "Your son, your stupid son. If I see the bastard, I'll shoot him myself."

The father apologized for the thoughtless actions of his son. Then with a half a smile he offered the cleaned up green bottle to the dock master.

The evil little king held it closer and tried to focus on the silt that settled to the bottom. With a slobbering laugh he tried to look intelligent as he said, "So, you think you can bribe me with this? You're going to need a whole lot more to get anywhere with me."

Then with an interested sneer he added, "This must mean that you are hiding your son."

Mario Senior said in a confident voice; "No, no. You can check my house, anytime."

The dock master gave him a cloudy look of doubt. This is exactly how Mario Senior wanted him to react. Over the years he noticed that whenever Warappo had to think too hard, he would look for another drink.

The dizzy dock master looked at the old green bottle again and said, "Ahh, Mojito." He fell back into his chair and popped the cork, then smelled the savory spices in the warm, pure alcohol.

He threatened the father with his dirty brown finger. "I'm watching your house! I'm watching you!" Then with a sly voice he said, "I'm watching your wife's ass, too!"

The father conjured his inner strength and ignored the torment with a smile that faded in and out on his strained face.

At the end of his morning on the boat and on the way home, Mario Senior turned his head towards the fish house. Butterflies took off in his gut as he saw Warappo slumped over out cold.

The magic green bottle had worked.

CS♥SO

His wife held the hand of their youngest as she left the house for what appeared to be a casual walk. She carried nothing with her.

A few minutes later the father and the older of the two daughters left from the back door.

The four met on the longer route to the boats. It went behind a thick patch of mangrove trees that cast a shadow on the dock and the family boat. The father had secretly cut a narrow path through the wall of tangled roots that rose from the shallow water. He pulled aside a few green branches that covered the entrance and the Family disappeared into the dense brush.

Each parent had a child on their back as they waded to the pilings behind the boat, just out of view from the fish house.

One by one, with quick and quiet motion, they crossed the dock and dropped down onto the deck. There was just enough room in the tiny cabin for the mother and the older daughter. The baby girl of the family smiled big when she got to sit on her daddy's lap and help him steer the boat.

They cast off the lines and idled in the direction of the fuel dock on the far side of the fish house.

When Mario Senior saw that Warappo was still out of it, he eased on by with a natural smile, tickling his Daughter.

Sometimes a rare magic will happen when a bold move is made in plain sight. It can hide in the cluttered activity of normalcy and just go unnoticed.

The daring act of the family deserved to succeed. They simply became invisible against the broad panorama of daylight.

The sleeping eyes of Los Villos had missed the easy escape. The few eyes that were open belonged to those who would never say a word.

From her kitchen window, Warappo's wife watched as the family boat entered into the swells of a friendly ocean. She stopped doing her housework long enough to dry her hands. Then with damp eyes, she blew a soft kiss in their direction.

CHAPTER 13
SHORTY'S BIG DAY

Like any kid who will count the days on his fingers, Shorty looked at his hands twice, with two more fingers to boot. He was in his morning hangout in the fly bridge, smelling the Harbor.

"Twenty-two frigging days," he said out loud.

Then he sheepishly looked around to make sure no one had heard him talking to himself.

He picked at the seal on a fresh bottle of cheap Cuban rum. He worked hard at looking like he was totally cool, with the poisonous wait. But not being mobile, and having too much time to think was taking his mind in too many crazy directions.

A few call-outs from some of the neighboring boats drove him to his feet to see what was going on.

He saw a gray government boat weaving through his neighborhood in the Flotilla. Standing on the bow was a bearded man holding a clip board; he seemed to be reading off the names of the boats as he passed.

Shorty tried not to set himself up for another gut punch of disappointment. Many of the other boats had been in the harbor longer than he had.

The Cuban official pointed to Shorty's stern and steered in his direction.

Shorty took the five-foot jump from the fly bridge to the bow and almost bounced off the boat. Then he jogged along the narrow gunwale to the stern and helped the Cuban officials tie off.

He remained quiet as his face flushed with the beginnings of a perfect feeling.

The serious and bland officer ignored the friendly invitations from the excited passengers to board. He looked straight at Shorty and asked in English, "Who is the captain of this vessel?"

Shorty stepped forward and proudly said; "I am."

The bearded man found Shorty's name next to the documentation of his boat. Then he handed Shorty three pages, stapled together. In a mechanical voice he said, "Have your boat tied off at the embarkation dock by noon."

Shorty ran his thumb down the list. None of the names jumped off of the pages as anyone he should recognize.

He smiled, when he handed it to Esperanza. "This is going to be interesting. One hundred and five—one hundred and nine including us—on this forty-five foot boat."

He looked at the sky for any hint of what the weather might bring. His wonderful mood combined with a sense of urgency when he saw the clock. He had less than an hour to reach the congested area around the loading docks.

His insides were vibrating with some newfound energy as he cranked up the motor. He couldn't wait to leave this long ordeal somewhere in the distant past.

But he put the brakes on because he knew well that the toughest times lay ahead. It would be an ominous crossing. The reality of being responsible for the lives of so many began to sober his excitement and lie heavy on his confidence. Shorty was now emotionally invested in the quest of bringing what People he could, and placing them on free soil.

He knew that soon his aching home sickness will be cured with the first blip, on the horizon, that would grow into the Key West skyline.

His busy momentum slowed when he noticed the happy face of Esperanza drop as she scanned the last page of the manifest.

Felicia and Eduardo politely helped the older lady hold the pages. They quietly read the names with the kind of anticipation that was hard to hold back. Twice they cheered as two of the names were from their list of family members. Then they went quiet with concern as Esperanza shook her head in disbelief and then she went over the list again. This time she read it slowly and methodically to herself, making sure she hadn't missed a name that would be precious to her.

Sympathetic hearts watched as the elegant older lady stood with her crushing disappointment. As though blind, she climbed the ladder down into the bunk area and slowly closed the hatch, to be alone.

Shorty continued his work, but his mind stayed on Esperanza. She seemed to have aged twenty years in the last few moments.

He knew that she had paid Dagger the lion's share of the cost to charter the boat. He saw her brave the unladylike conditions of the rough fishing boat with an easy-going style. Her concerns were always for everyone else. Now this hard journey would be without any reward for her. The family members who she wanted to bring home gave in to the fear of retaliation against the ones they would have to leave behind.

Shortly quietly cussed the general, all-around unfairness of life.

Before he pulled the hook to head to the staging area, he opened the heavy hatch cover of the ice hold with the toe of his boot. He pulled out two boxes of coiled trap rope and gave Eduardo a quick lesson on how to tie a simple net knot. It was his plan to create a net, with large mesh, around the open part of the deck, and attach it to the canopy brace. It would be secured to the gunwale and would serve to keep the humanity, from being thrown from the boat if the ocean chose to be unforgiving.

Then he pulled out two large aluminum pots that were normally used to par cook the stone crab biters that are harvested along with the lobster. He wiped them out with a paper towel and then gave them to Felicia. He asked her to secure them on the gas burners of the stove, and cook their remaining rice. He reminded her that these people would be hungry. But if they were given too much food, too quickly, their bodies could reject it. He also knew that once they entered the swells of the open ocean the refugees would become sick anyway. But they needed to eat something for a little more strength to make the long, hard crossing.

Before he cast off to head for the dock where he would be loaded with his Human cargo. Shorty went down to the bunks to check on his motherly friend. She was lying on one of the cushions with her arm over her forehead, staring at the ceiling.

He touched her shoulder, startling her out of a sad dream state. Her eyes that usually sparked with clarity were now welled up with cloudy tears.

Shorty had to try hard to not shed a tear of his own. He paused before he said anything. He wasn't really sure what he could say. Before he could try to console her with his words, she cupped both of her hands around his big hand and pulled it to her face.

"Come on, my Captain, let's bring these people home with us. They will make good Americans."

He helped her up and they came back out on the deck with a fresh wind behind their backs.

For a long while, he could feel the wet of her tears soak into his callused hand.

His stance was stiff as he steered past the two Russian gunboats that guarded the mouth of Mariel Harbor. From in between their bows, Shorty caught a glimpse of the ocean and the distant whitecaps offshore. He took in a deep breath of worry. Then he looked ahead to the first long dock that pierced the belly of the harbor. He nervously watched the ever-circling ring of scavenger birds.

He pointed the boat towards three guards who waved him over. They held their AKs with the strap around the elbow for a quick response. As he tied off, they handed him an official-looking form that he had to sign. Then they told him to stay with his boat and wait.

Three other boats laid along the side of the loading dock.

Shorty took a stronger breath when he noticed that his buddy Pots was among them. They would make a natural team to survive the troubling miles ahead.

He shut the motor down to save fuel. Then he joined Eduardo in finishing the safety net. It was clumsy to attach, but when it was lashed to the boat both men looked at each other and nodded their approval. It would have to work.

The strong fiberglass work boats were designed to carry a full load of heavy water-soaked lobster traps with little stress, even in the face of a challenging sea. But the broad flat bottoms with a keel were designed for the more shallow inshore waters. The deep water out in the Gulf Stream would have the long swells, which demanded a heavy boat to travel into the waves. If they were to fall sideways into the trough, this could roll the boat. Fiberglass might be strong, but it would sink like a rock. They would have to keep the boat moving forward and making way to remain safe. Doing this would take constant concentration to stay on course.

As the preparations were winding down, Shorty jumped to the dock to pull a fresh water hose onto the deck and top off the drinking water.

Shorty looked over to the next boat where Pots had his feet up on his captain's chair, sucking down a cold one.

With a dimply, closed-mouth smile, Shorty flipped the bird to his friend.

Pots leaned forward and laughed. "Fuck you, too, ya big lummox." Then he crumbled the empty beer can and acted like he was going to throw it at Shorty.

Typical for the young brotherhood of lobster men. They could laugh off any nervousness or fears they might have. At least when they were in front of each other.

Commercial fishermen choose a life of risk. But the thought of dying at sea was always buried somewhere in the back of their minds. It seldom became a part of any conversation.

Shorty took his binoculars up in the fly bridge for a better look around. He reached for the unopened bottle of rum, then paused. *Na, this shit will just make me tired, and it looks like it's gonna be a long time before I can sleep.*

Then he remembered the little stash of pot that he had stuffed in the pocket of his shorts back on the first day. He went down below and fished it out of the dirty clothes. Then he rolled a fat one and climbed up to be alone on the bridge.

He figured he had come this far without getting into any trouble, and the Guards seemed to be out of smelling range. So he fired it up and held it like he would hold a cigarette. Then he smoked it down. When he finished, he crumbled the roach, and tossed it in the garbage-strewn water.

Once in a while, he had to tempt fate, just a little bit.

He began to check out the two other boats that were a part of his group.

One was an old-school Cuban fishing boat. It had a cement hull and sat low in the water. It looked like it had been recently restored and painted. There was no telling what kind of shape the motor was in. The name on the stern was familiar, and he believed that it belonged to one of the families who had a popular business in down town Key West. His first thought was that it was too narrow and not a good choice to carry any weight across the Straits. As he continued to look, he felt a strange burn inside; then a cold chill ran up his backbone, ending at the nape of his neck. It left a slight metallic taste in his mouth.

Something didn't feel right, but he couldn't grasp the problem. He would have worry about this one.

The other boat that was tied off on the end of the dock was an eye-catching sport fishing boat. It was at least a sixty-footer and seemed to be dressed out with all the bells and whistles that an expensive yacht could have.

Shorty was a boat lover, but the only experience he had was with the rough and relatively uncomfortable work boats. Often times he would leaf through the boating magazines and ogle over the extreme vessels with all the opulence and technology that could be had. It was another dream of his to someday pilot such a fine craft.

His attention was turned toward the land with the anticipation of seeing the people who would soon be boarding his boat. He leaned into the binoculars to better see the green canvas tents under the drooping Cuban flag.

The one with the Red Crescent seemed to be a medical facility of some sort. He wondered why the Red Cross seemed to avoid this crazy Communist country so close to the United States.

There appeared to be a good number of Americans milling around the staging area. They gathered in groups among the tents; some fell into lines. There was a muffled, barking sound of frustrating negotiations. Shorty imagined southern drawls and New

York accents banging up against the animated, loud Spanish. He assumed that everyone had a different, problem with the clumsy processing of so many humans. And everyone's problem was the most urgent.

The afternoon was sliding away and he was speeding with anxious energy to get started. At least a few hours of daylight would give him a secure start to the impending voyage. He was tempted to walk over to the confusion and see what the hold up was. But he took firm orders, that came in a threatening tone from a particularly tiny guard who looked like a toy. He and his passengers were to stay with the boat until they were contacted.

Shorty was reluctant to bring any last-minute attention his way.

He had just noticed a few dozen American boats that appeared to be impounded in a rocky cove just north of the staging area. Some had been pulled up onto the small beach. It hit Shorty that these were the ones that had been confiscated—probably for some small offense or trumped-up reason.

With a tinge of anger, he watched as a tall balding officer sat in the captain's chair of a fine-looking crawfish boat from Marathon Key. With a conceited smile, he lit up a long, fat cigar and admired his new possession.

Shorty thought about the owner and crew and felt bad for their loss. This close to the end was no time to screw up.

He was sitting just under the edge of the spooky flock of vultures. Looking up, he could see that they were focused on a spot that was on the other side of the hill. They were falling and rising just out of sight. He remembered that this is where the line of refugees that he saw on his day in Havana seemed to originate.

He caught the occasional scent of something he couldn't quite place. It was septic, mixed with carrion, and it made a sticky burn in his sinus.

The crest of that hill seemed to have the most guards, and they stood armed. A few looked down on the staging area, but most faced the hidden mystery beyond the hill.

Shorty was jerked from out of his thinking and taken over by a sick feeling. His eyes picked out of the crowd the familiar outline of Flaco's Afro. His long-awaited day seemed to be going smoothly until the thin man started down the dock towards the boat. He was talking loudly and pointing to some paper with two of the guards, including the undersized man with the oversized gun.

Shorty's stomach burned as Flaco approached with a phony cautiousness.

As each of the passengers noticed the return of the man they thought that they were rid of, they threw up their arms in surrender.

Flaco opened up with false poise and showed a sorry smirk. He offered an overly formal apology to the folded arms and searing face of Esperanza.

The two guards seemed to enjoy the proud-to-be-an-asshole act that the thin man used on the American captain and his Cuban-American passengers.

Shorty stepped in between the invasive group and his boat with a protective aura.

Flaco said with a mocking smile, "Hey, my friends, I'm back from my vacation and anxious to rejoin you." He tilted his head to the side. "Aren't you glad to see me again?"

Then he went to step up on the boat.

Shorty moved in front of him and held out his big paws. "Hey, hey, wait a minute there, boy. Where do you think you're going?"

Flaco snapped his finger and pointed to the guard holding the paper. Then he said, "Look, Chiquedico, it says right here that I came into the harbor on this boat." He pointed to the deck at Shorty's feet. "I have to return with my four family members on this same boat. If you have a problem with this, then you can gripe to these guys about it." He gestured over his shoulder at the amused guards.

With a question on his face, Shorty turned to his passengers, looking for a way out of submitting to this miserable change of plan.

Esperanza spoke in a low, serious manner. "Better do what they want, and let him on. They could make a big deal out of this."

Shorty dropped his shoulder and stepped aside with the wary look of resignation.

Flaco came back on board and made himself at home. He admired the safety net and nodded his approval. He had the air of someone who was inspecting his future property. He continued reacquainting with the boat, but avoided the leery eyes of the passengers.

Shorty had Eduardo ask the Guards how much longer it would be before they could begin loading.

After a few minutes of rapid-fire Spanish with the gun-stroking military men, Eduardo could only tell him, "They won't commit to a time. We just have to remain patient."

The guards stayed close to the boat for a while. When they saw no further problem, they walked down to the end of the dock to look at the yacht.

CHAPTER 14
THE BOY WITH A BROKEN ARM

On the eve of the end, hard feelings had returned to the boat.

The passengers went quiet as they worked on turning rice and beans into a soup that would help to rehydrate the suffering refugees. They looked for anything else that could be done to accommodate the forthcoming masses.

Flaco buried his face in a week-old newspaper. He occasionally piped in a whistle to an off-key song that skipped on a scratchy groove in his head.

Reluctantly Shorty had to reopen his other set of eyes. The intuitive ones that he kept stashed in the back of his skull. It was the extra effort he needed to make in order to share the boat space with a man who tested him, at every turn. But now, at least, he was aware of the motivation behind Flaco's attitude.

Shorty appeared to be the only thing that stood in his way to take over the boat. If he could rattle the young man and cause him to make mistakes, it would help him sway the old captain to shift his boat from fishing to drug smuggling.

Shorty already knew that Dagger was angry because he had kept his boat two weeks longer then they had planned. He was also well aware that the added risk and worry was his responsibility. He hated it when the feisty old bulldog was mad. More than a few times, he had to pull him off of some drunk sailor in some sandy-floored bar. He had an old-fashioned temperament and slamming it out was always a possibility.

He could almost feel the painful vibrations emitting from the old captain from all the way across the ocean. It made his temples burn to think about explaining everything when he got home.

It would break Shorty's heart if his captain lost faith in him. This job was his only real plan for the future. It was the best opportunity, he might ever have. Everything about his current life depended on his relationship with Dagger. But now, he was beginning to feel his true power, and saw the thin man as the only thing standing in his way.

He returned to the bridge to see what was going on around him. The day was getting old, and his urgency returned like a force.

Through the wavy mirage of heat, he noticed a few heads in the staging area turn towards the crest of the hill.

From under the savage birds, a single file line of battered people limped down toward the loading dock. They were prodded by the tormenting guards, who considered them traitors and deserters.

As they came into view, Shorty let his eyes rest on each one. He tried his best to read their individual stories. His excitement was invaded by that strange emotion—the one that he had felt on the day he saw the swimmer suffer the gaff hook. Part fear and part anger, with each fighting for the bat to slam him in the stomach.

As he watched his people, there was something ominous, something bigger, than the world that lived inside of his mind. This energy gathered and carried him forward.

Reality stings when it declares a man responsible for the lives of one hundred and eight human beings. Shorty almost caught himself praying.

Instead, he looked to the sky, then over to the ocean side. He turned his head to face the same direction as the compass bearing he would use to reach his home, which lay just over the horizon.

Then he noticed that the highest, wispy white clouds were moving in a different direction than the gentle wind that poured past him.

Sensing a sea change was coming, he openly begged the Gulf Stream for mercy on this night.

When the line was halted next to the cabin, the little toy guard with the big attitude made everyone continue to stand and, in his words, enjoy the heat. When they spoke or moaned, too loud, he would point his assault weapon to keep the fear alive in the wide-eyed refugees.

Now Shorty was within a few feet of his precious cargo. Every face near the boat was looking straight at him. He could almost feel a little stage fright. At first they didn't know what to make of the American captain with the ugly, orange boots. He eased their worries with a smile and gave eye contact to each one as he looked down the grim line.

He admired their sand, for living and surviving under the guns of this government. He thought that it must be a rare sort of courage to leave under the threat of those same guns. Many of the Cuban people wanted to leave but were too afraid to join with this unprecedented mass migration. These people were different. They had had enough. This would be a dangerous gamble. It would be the only chance, in their lifetime, to find a free life. They continued to trudge through the foggy unknown for the privilege of living in the United States.

Which was still the unknown.

Some were helping to hold up the weaker or elderly people, who staggered in the line that stretched back over and beyond the Hill. Shorty guessed that the elders were passing through the exhaustion by remembering the prosperous and free Cuba of history. Perhaps they knew someone state side who could help them finish out their lives as free people.

So many children, he thought. Complete families, huddled together and contained by the Soldiers in the straight, hot line. A guilty, but pragmatic, thought of less weight and more room on the boat, crossed his mind.

Shorty rose with a fatherly concern when he heard the crying voice of an infant. His eyes found the mother who shielded her baby and breast from the murderous sun. Her three daughters, who had long black hair and big round eyes, leaned against her. They appeared to be a year or two apart in age, and wore dresses made from the same bolt of cloth. The father stood over his beautiful family with a carved, serious face.

A short way into the line, Shorty focused in on a white pile of dreadlocks, swaying back and forth in the land breeze. It gave him a wild image of snow, in blatant defiance of the Tropics.

She was an older woman with ebony skin, dressed in bright African colors. Her bare, leathery feet stepped in place to an imaginary rhythm. Her lips seemed to be whispering a song as she smiled, eyes closed, her face in the sun. He was taken with her spirit and would call her Snow Flake.

The toy guard looked up at Shorty in his fly bridge and took in a red-faced breath. He tried to look mean and menacing. But Shorty just smiled at him with a sassy look of confidence.

The toy guard quickly looked away, and showed a hint of intimidation from the strong, free American who was looking down on him.

Now the worried faces became open-faced smiles that looked at him without fear. His quiet and smart defiance to the authority figure gave them all a new hope. This would be the man who would deliver them to a better life.

Shorty wasn't even aware that he was having a rock star moment. Instead he was taking notice of how many were touching their dry, swollen lips and muttering the word agua. Water.

The toy guard took a slow walk toward the land and continued to enjoy his job of intimidation. Shorty watched as he unscrewed the hose on the dock and took it away from the hands of the thirsty. He smiled and coiled it up, leaving it useless. When he walked away, a few of the children went for the few drops beading up on the planks.

After a long half an hour of waiting, people beginning to drop from where they stood.

The big American couldn't take it anymore. He knew the guards were serious when they told him to stay on his boat. But he had plenty of fresh water on board. This would not do! He remembered a conversation he had overheard in Havana. He learned that the Cuban government had issued orders to the guards and soldiers to go easy on the Americans. They were also told to keep any violence against the refugees hidden from the news cameras, and the eyes of all foreigners. This would only provoke a more serious response from the world community.

Shorty believed that these uniformed bimbos could do little harm to him—at least not for sharing his water. These people were sick from thirst and getting worse in front of his eyes.

Most of the guards were now concentrated in the shade near the entrance of the dock. They appeared lazy and bored with the daily herding and loading of humans.

Shortly went below and pulled up a plastic five-gallon bottle of store-bought water from the ice hold. The weight from the dead lift woke up his injury from the great storm. Still, he handled the heavy jug with his good arm and peeled the seal off as he left the boat.

Before his passengers knew what he was up to, he was out on the dock, doling out the sweet taste of life. Shorty looked over his shoulder as he made his way down the line. He knew that this might trigger a response. Nervous, he would now find out how much of a response they would make.

No more than ten people received a pan of water before the toy guard and two of his partners came running back down the dock.

As the guards approached, Shorty did what he did best. He just played stupid, then smiled at the toy guard and he continued with his effort.

The tiny man raised his rifle and prepared to bring the butt end down on the American's back. But one of the other Guards put his hand up and shook his head. Begrudgingly, the toy guard stood down, but not without putting a hard tap on Shorty's injured shoulder. He was lucky enough to hit right where the sore spot was.

Shorty ignored the pain as he stood to face the authorities. He managed to keep the smile going, even though he was shedding his fear and growing his anger.

The guard who stopped the rifle butt began to speak in the Cuban slang. He said something about big cojones and chuckled. Then his face went firm as he ordered the big American back on his boat.

Shorty remained agreeable and showed his hands to now be empty. "No problem. No problema."

Then he left the water and stepped one foot back on the boat.

When he turned he saw the defeated look come back onto the faces of the refugees.

The guards laughed as they tipped the big jug and rolled it off the dock. It bobbed with the floating trash of the harbor. Then they used the flat of their weapons to straighten the line back to the rigid, cramping wait.

Shorty's passengers helped him back on board and gave him quiet thanks for trying to help. They gently reminded the emotionally charged Shorty to try and be patient. They reassured him that when the orders came and the people were on the boat, they could give them, whatever they needed.

Shorty saw Flaco's smirk, which was meant to mock his little run-in with the guards. He decided that the best place to be was back up on the bridge once again, where he could try to stay out of trouble and put his mind on the tough trip ahead.

He started counting and configuring the people and their placement on the boat. It would make the most sense to put the elderly, and the weakest-looking down in the bunk area, and up in the front. Though it would be confined and cause most of them to become seasick, it would be dry during what promised to be a wet crossing. The middle of the boat, on the deck and engine box, would be the best for children and their parents. Some of the breaking waves might soak them, but it was the best he could do. He was nervous about keeping the little ones on the boat.

Around the sides and at the stern would be wet for most of the trip. He reserved these areas for young men who were healthy enough to attempt standing. Among this group, he noticed a few who looked different from the rest. They had shaved heads and tattoos. He knew right away that they must be some of the convicts that Castro was planting on each boatload of people. The very back of the stern would be the best for these folks.

In the distance, and on top of the ridge, Shorty's eyes were drawn to a man holding his son.

He leaned into his binoculars to see the veins on the man's neck, straining under the weight of his child, who looked limp and unconscious. This father wobbled, anguish pouring from his face.

As Shorty strained to see better his heart began to rattle in his chest.

In the future, when he remembered this moment, he would never remember pushing past the warnings of his passengers, his long legs quickly putting his boat and the dock behind him. Oblivious to the orders to stay on board, he reached the collapsing father in time to help ease the boy onto the dirt.

The restricted area sign was now behind him.

He found a pulse on the boy's neck. His skin was dry and cool, but not cold.

Now on his knees, and holding the nine-year-old boy, he saw that his arm hung in an unnatural way. The wet, red towel that was wrapped on his upper arm, showed the outline of a shard of bone.

Shorty was now shaking and fighting off nausea. His head looked back and forth, not knowing what he should do, or which way he should turn.

The father glazed over, and stared, unblinking at the big American.

Looking down from the ridge, Shorty saw the tent with the Red Crescent a few dozen yards away.

Thankfully the boy was passed out and beyond his pain. But Shorty winced as he secured the badly broken arm with his hand. Then he slowly stood up and adjusted his hold so he could make it down to the medical tent without jarring the compound fracture.

When his legs straightened out, he was facing the other side of the mysterious hill. His eyes opened wide and his mouth hung loose as he was now looking at what the American eyes were not meant to see.

Under the circling vultures, a vast network of stockyards surrounded by razor wire fence filled his view.

The stench burned his eyes as they blinked into the reality of what he was seeing. These were the animal pens of what they called Mosquito Bay. This is where a well-trained rifle butt had broken the arm of the boy. This is also where the infant child had been born.

Many thousands of people were contained, with no cover from the cancerous sun. They stood or lay down in the mud of their own waste.

Some would wait here for weeks.

He could hear the low, alto drone of human voices. A sad bass tone of suffering, combined with the hum of flies and the caws of the scavenger birds. It all came together to make a sad harmony, a song of death.

Frozen silent, he forced his head to turn slightly to a barrage of screams close to one side of the fence. Two Guards manned a fire hose and sprayed it over the masses. When the people jammed up closer, to catch some of the water, the guards used the force of the stream to drive some of the old ones off their feet and to the ground.

Shorty could not grasp the laughter-driven abuse. Then his blood cooled when he noticed the rows of black body bags laid out on the other side of the dreadful fence.

He snapped himself out of his weightlessness and looked down at the dazed Father

In his bold but shakey voice Shorty said; "Come with me. Dalle. Let's go".

Shorty turned to face the sights of five AK 47s.

Helpless, and believing his life was lost, he slowly turned his back to the anxious guns. He stroked the boy's forehead and hoped the bullets would miss the child.

He heard no shots but a second or two later he felt the slam on his shoulder. It was as though his injury was a bright red target. He almost dropped the boy, but he managed to straighten up again.

Unable to think, only react, Shorty turned and walked right through the muzzles of the guns. Two of the guards fell like bowling pins, and the others parted in shock from the big American's bold maneuver.

He brushed aside a British news crew and their cameras— probably the only reason the Guards had not pulled the triggers. His long legs made short the distance to the safety of the medical tent.

The toy guard and his friends had to run to keep up. They were panting and spitting profanity at the determined American, who left their Noise behind him.

Shorty's only thought was to keep the boy's arm from parting during the fast, rough walk. He pushed his way past the line and through the entrance of the medical tent. Then he found an open cot and gently laid the boy on the white sheet.

An Eastern-looking doctor and two veiled nurses with dark Asian eyes now hovered over the boy.

The Guards were stopped at the front flap of the tent. There was debate among them about what to do next. Shorty put his hands behind his head and surrendered. When he came outside they tried to handcuff him. But he refused, knowing that having his hands restrained behind his back would send him to the ground in a panic. He nodded in an agreeable way for them to show him the way.

The Guards were surprisingly uncomfortable with being the center of everyone's attention, so they didn't push the cuffs. They didn't seem to want this particular duty and appeared to be anxious to return to the shade.

All except the toy guard, who was determined to defeat the big American with any charges he could bring.

CHAPTER 15
THE DOOFUS

They put the tiny man in charge and he poked and prodded the big American to the green tent, under the heavy Cuban flag that drooped even with a breeze. This place seemed to be the center of the failing logistics for the whole event.

Shorty looked over towards the dock and told himself that Eduardo would be able to handle Dagger's boat if he were to be punished or detained. Then he noticed that most everyone at the staging area was looking at him. Some were openly praising his actions and others ushered him past with eyes of amazement. This made him feel righteous for doing whatever crime they would decide to charge him with. He followed the toy guard and almost felt a little shy from being the object of so many eyes.

Once inside, he ran head on into the end of a short line that lead to a long table. When he stopped, the toy guard crammed into his back with his rifle between them.

All together there were three tables handling the endless problems. The noise startled him back into reality. Under the loud steel fans was the clatter of typewriters and the chatter of radio communications. Dozens of passionate conversations between the rattled Americans and the irritated officials vibrated in Shorty's ears.

Each time the line moved forward, the toy guard pushed from behind. It was all that Shorty could do to keep from challenging this nuisance. He hung his head low and worried more about Dagger's boat than himself.

A man with dandruff on a greasy head of hair was now the only one between Shorty and the impatient-looking official seated at the table. Beads of sweat ran down the official's brow, even in the wind, from the fans.

A slightly sandy and almost sultry woman's voice cut through the collective noise and captured his attention away from the impending drilling. Curious, Shortly looked over at the next table. There was the familiar, back of the beautiful Latina.

His sweat went dry, replaced with goose bumps.

He turned his face and hoped that she wouldn't see the big dumb gringo, the same one she caught staring at her in Havana. He would be so embarrassed for her to see him the captive of this gooney little man. But he mustered up his courage and once again found himself looking at her back side. Her long hair rippled down over a halter top and to the waist of her faded, cut-off jeans.

She was in an animated conversation with the official at her table. Shorty tried to make out what she was saying, but it was too much Spanish for him to understand.

From this close, he could see her eye lashes move above a flirtatious smile. She seemed to be charming her way to something. Her movements and speech, were smooth and she appeared to be winning the negotiation.

She leaned toward the table and the enraptured official. With a sweet smile, she handed him an envelope. Then she turned to her side to wait for his response.

When She saw the big gringo, she appeared to look right through him, like he wasn't there.

For a second, Shorty was relieved that he was not recognizable to her, so he offered a polite smile.

Then she rolled her eyes and, in a violated way, she quickly turned back to the table.

Crap, Shorty thought. This was the second time this lady had seen him as a doofus. Like he was some sort of school boy who stares at beautiful girls.

He put his hand on the burning in his stomach and moved up to the table. Embarrassed, he tried to focus on the business at hand.

The toy guard had already gone into a rapid-fire set of accusations. The language was impossible for him to keep up with.

The official pulled at both ends of his pencil and stared at the big American.

Shorty strained to catch and translate a word here and there. None of it made any sense to him, and now he was paralyzed, without a way to defend himself. He didn't stand a chance.

When he was offered an opportunity to speak up for himself, he could only say, "Yo lo siento. I'm sorry. Por favor, Yo vamoose de me boate.

Please let me go back to my boat. At least, that's what he hoped he'd said.

The official and the toy guard looked at Shorty and his fractured attempt at speaking Spanish, like he was from Outer Space.

Then it happened. Shorty didn't know where it came from, but he said it, "Look, you little cocksuckers, let me go back to my boat."

The toy guard looked confused, but the official dropped his pencil and said in perfect English, "That was a really stupid thing to say to me. I was going to let you go, but now I'm not sure."

Between gritted teeth, Shorty said, "Oh, shit."

Then the official's gaze shifted and he beamed a big smile.

A soft but firm little hand lifted Shorty's arm up and over her shoulder. She gave him an affectionate hug and patted him on his chest. The voice rang in his ear as Rosa took over the failing conversation.

Fumbling to contain his shock, he looked down at her with no belief that this was really happening.

When he went to say something, she quickly pinched the quick of his arm. Then she tugged on his hair and pulled his head down to her mouth. She whispered softly in his ear, "Shut the fuck up."

Shorty opened his eyes wide and obeyed.

She spoke so quickly it was hard for Shorty to follow the conversation. But even with his limited Spanish he could make out a few key phrases. Something about Este amigo mio, and el gringo estúpido.

That seemed pretty clear, even to Shorty.

Whatever else she was saying seemed to have the official changing his attitude. Then she reached into the edge of her blouse and plucked out a tightly folded wad of greenbacks and slipped it into the hand of the mesmerized man behind the table.

While she paid the acceptable bribe, she also gave a hard poke with her sharp elbow into the ribs of the stupefied big gringo.

The jab helped him wake up out of his helplessness. The girl of his dreams was actually paying him some attention, even if it was only with a painful gesture.

Then he put on a sorry smile and he mouthed the sound, "Ooouw." For her sake, he made sure that it came out sounding exaggerated and a little silly.

The official flipped two fingers in the direction of the entrance and then waved for the next people problem in the line.

Shorty didn't realize it was over with and went to say something.

In one quick movement, Rosa slipped out from under his arm and spun him around. She put her claws into his triceps and dragged him out through the entrance of the tent.

When they emerged, she began to walk away without saying another word.

As she let go of his arm, Shorty had enough presence of mind to slide his hand down to hers. He thought she might pull away but instead she slowed and gripped his rough but gentle hand. It was that moment that Rosa gave Shorty her first smile. Still not saying a word, she lead him to a quiet, less crowded area in between the tie ropes of the tents When the Latina stopped and turned her face to him, she had to look up, to see his eyes.

This was the first time he could clearly see her face. The gold flecks in her light brown eyes captured his brain and emptied it of everything but her.

The rushes that consumed him were threatening to turn into the shakes but just sharing the same air seemed to warm his insides and it began to calm his nerves.

He made an attempt to find something cool or intelligent to say. As usual, when he was face to face with a pretty girl, he began to draw a blank.

Rosa sensed the shyness of this rugged-looking man, and she kind of liked it. So She cocked her head to the side and opened up a conversation by asking, "How tall are you, anyway?"

Shorty continued to stay in those eyes for a few more seconds, and slowly evolved into a natural smile. Rosa grew her own smile, and said, "What?" Then she started to giggle.

His thinking fell back to almost normal and he answered, "Oh, I'd say about eight foot six inches. By the way you happen to be, ahh, let's see, only about the three thousandth person to ask me that very question."

In a playful and challenging way, Rosa put her hand on her hip and said, "So, the big gringo seems to be brave, now he thinks he has a sense of humor."

Shorty glanced away from her teasing, then began shaking his head from side to side. Then he said with a purpose, "Wait, wait, a minute.

Her smile was taken back, but just a little.

Then he made a short, polite bow and extended his hand. "People call me Shorty. Some of my Cuban-American friends call me Chiquitico. I guess that sort of means the same thing. Kind of a parody on my tallness."

Rosa blushed a bit for forgetting about the introduction. She was also feeling flattered, with the polite greeting.

Usually Men were either too bold and conquering or just intimidated when they approached her. But this guy seemed polite and interesting.

She said, "Oh my goodness, I'm sorry. Where are my manners?" She took his big hand and gave it a good shake, followed by a sly smile.

Rosa put her finger on her lip and looked at him like she was trying to place him from somewhere in her past. Even though she knew exactly where she had seen this man before. Then She gave out a recognizing kind of laugh.

"Ah! Didn't I see you back in Havana a few days ago? Weren't you the guy in the window of the Triton hotel. The one who stared at my back side so hard that it burned? Do you realize that you interrupted my socializing?"

She crossed her arms and waited for an admission of guilt, from the flabbergasted Shorty. He hesitated, then rebounded by saying, "Wow! You mean my eyes can actually burn someone's butt. I never realized I had such super powers. I'm gonna have to figure out how to work this thing. It might just come in handy. Who knows, maybe I can even start fires and light cigarettes."

She laughed openly and began looking for a place to sit. There was a gray, splintery board next to two toppled five-gallon buckets.

When she went to fix the makeshift bench, Shorty took over. Then he held it as she scooted sideways and sat Indian style.

Then he straddled the board, so they were facing each other, with some respectful space in between them.

"I've got to give you a big thanks," he said. "Whatever you said back there was amazing. I thought I was in the worst kind of trouble, until you came along to my rescue."

He watched as she schooched onto the bench. He had to make an effort not to let his eyes linger on her deeply tanned legs.

"Why would you help me out like that? You don't know me from Adam, and it was a big risk for you."

Then he remembered the bribe. "Oh, darn." He reached into his pocket for some cash.

Rosa reached over and touched his arm. "No, no, don't bother. No, really, I have you to thank."

Now Shorty was flat out perplexed.

"I saw what you did for the boy." She gently squeezed his forearm. "Other people saw his condition but were afraid to do anything about it. You did the right thing, and I couldn't watch you be punished for it."

Shorty looked back to the hill above Mosquito Bay, then to the tent with the Red Crescent.

"Ah, the boy." He shook his head. "If the boy lives, what do you think will happened to him and his father?"

Rosa's friendly face went sad and said; "I just don't know." Her eyes began to look wet and shiny. "I was born in this country. Now it seems like it's been turned inside out."

Shorty saw the pain begin to stain her beauty, so he eased their minds into another direction. "So, Rosa, where do you call home?" As soon as he spoke, a waft of rotten rubber smell emitted from his dank boots and rose up to his nose.

Holy crap. He tried not to look down at the source, and hoped it might go in a direction other than hers. He offered a childish smile at her and casually reached down to fold the top of his boot over and held it against his leg. As if this would really stop her from experiencing his embarrassing stink.

Rosa hadn't noticed yet. She began talking about her life in Jupiter, Florida. She reached across the bench to point out her family-built Pleasure Craft on the end of the loading dock. When she did, her face was right above his boots. She went quiet and rumpled her eyebrows. Then her face went grim as she looked at a nearby trash can and anything else that might smell bad.

Then she pointed to his ugly orange boots.

He ground his teeth and, like a ventriloquist, squeezed out the words, "Oh, God."

Busted once again. "Rosa, I want you to meet my pet boots. Believe it or not, I give these guys a good bath twice a year. Whether they need it or not."

Then he went serious and explained that he was a crawfisherman, and these were his old work boots. Somehow he had forgotten to bring a real pair of shoes. Then he reached down with both hands, to hold them shut. He turned his comical face up to her to continue with the conversation.

When she saw him in his ridiculous discomfort, she fanned the air in front of her face. She blurted out, "Pee-yew!" Then she fell into hysterics.

Shorty felt like running away and jumping into the ocean. At this moment, he would have swum his way back home. He was sure now that she would get up and walk away from such a grubby man.

But Rosa kept pulling her surprises. Once again, she put her hand on his arm and smiled into his eyes.

"It's OK. My cousin over in Naples is also a lobster man. I helped him on the boat for years, and I must say, I'm familiar with stinky boot syndrome. I totally get it."

Shorty looked at her with a question in his eyes. Seeing reassurance there, he let go of the aromatic boots, sat up straight and then he leaned back. He felt devoured by his own embarrassment, until he began to laugh along with her.

If this didn't scare her off, he thought, *maybe there was more to this girl than I first thought.*

She laughed so hard that she teared up. With a folded paper napkin from her back pocket, she dried her eyes and said to him. "Mr Shorty, I'm not laughing at you. It's just that this is the first good laugh I've had since I've been here. Brave man, funny man and now stinky man.

Then she began to handle his embarrassment in a gentle way and settled into a more serious tone. She actually moved a little closer to him on the bench. With a slight tremble in her voice, she confided in him, "This whole trip has been so hard." The wear and disappointment from her ordeal in the harbor began to seep through her pretty face.

When he saw that this lady could go from laughter to almost a tear so quickly, he began to feel very protective of her. He realized that this woman was genuine and passionate.

Shorty began asking about the fine boats she built. Of course, he was amazed, and she was proud to describe the process.

He felt inspired with her story of coming to the United States, especially the part about her father working his way up into the American dream. But when she began talking about retrieving her brother and how difficult it had been, his thoughts went to his passenger Esperanza. To come this far and spend so much Heart, only to fail at saving family truly affected Shorty. He had a gut feeling that her brother wasn't going to make it. But he didn't express anything, other than encouragement. He gave her a big dose of his natural optimism.

She also hung on every word of his stories. His hitchhiking trips around the country and landing in Key West, of all places. A land lover who became a lobster man, and now shared the same love for the ocean that she always had.

Rosa told him that Key West was always on her map, and she had a few friends there.

She even shared a family recipe for crawfish and stone crab. When he mentioned playing the guitar, her interest was really tweaked. They spoke of music and agreed on much of what they liked.

Shorty was also honest about his relationship with Kim Sue. He still had to believe that everything would be the same when he got back home. With all of his worries and doubts, he was committed. He wouldn't know how to pretend to be anything different. After all, this was only a conversation with someone he would probably never see again. But he was still honored to share the same bench with a lady like her.

Rosa also admitted to having a boyfriend back home, then quickly changed the subject.

She came from a world of opulence. Only the very wealthy could patronize her family's business. As her family was proud of achieving the upper middle class, they lived modestly. She worked alongside her father and uncle and felt more comfortable around the working people who built boats. But socially, Rosa had been thrust into the rich kid scene in South Florida. She could never get used to interacting with young people who never seemed to have a job. She knew that she had been blessed with what people called natural beauty. But it never occurred to her to be conceited or too taken with herself. She was always honest, open, and friendly.

Most of the girls in her crowd were rude and whiny. Sometimes she was hurt from their meanness, and being left out of their friendships. The sting of jealousy was an unfair part of her life.

Many young men would approach her and put on the face of overconfidence. They would act macho and always seemed arrogant to Rosa. She found little attraction to boys who had too many toys and too little character. Soft hands and phony eyes were always reaching for her. But the young lady had too many natural qualities to find true love in this environment.

Just like Shorty, she also had a lot of doubts about her current boyfriend. On the day before she left, Rosa overheard him talking to one of his friends. He referred to her as a nice accessory to be seen riding in his new sports car.

For her to live a shallow life of boasting about wealth and social climbing would be impossible.

Rosa would never be anyone's trophy wife. Her idea of Mr. Right would simply be a real man—one who could be just as sensitive as he was strong.

She thought it was refreshing to be talking to a young working guy like Shorty. He seemed to be the right combination of confident and humble. She liked the fact that he could make the best out of a bad situation.

Though the conversation was brief, it was honest, and memorable.

For two strangers to meet and confide in the midst of such a difficult and dramatic event was healing to both.

Rosa took notice of some of the refugees in the line at Shorty's boat. They were beginning to stir, and their faces were turning ahead.

She touched his arm. "Well, Mr. Shorty, it looks like you finally get to go home."

Knowing about his long frustration with the waiting, she was glad to be the one to say the words.

In half a second, he was on his feet and facing the dock. He watched as the tired line began to move.

Then he turned to Rosa with his biggest smile and said, "It's about time." Then in a cowboy voice, he hooted, "Yee-haw!"

He looked back at the line, just to make sure that it was really happening.

When he turned to say his goodbye, she was staring ahead and seemed to be in a deep thought. He extended his hand. Rosa took it with both of her hands and broke out her own big smile. She uncrossed her legs and he helped her stand up from the bench.

As they faced each other, Shorty had a strong urge to open his arms for a hug, but he hesitated.

She also moved a little closer, but stopped short of contact.

She lived in Jupiter, Florida, and he lived all the way down in Key West. They had two completely different lives. Both were in other relationships. Surely there was no reason to think that there would be a future time together.

But Shorty couldn't accept the possibility of never seeing her again. He reached deep into his courage and, with shaky confidence, said, "Look, Rosa, I know we just met, and you don't know me very well but would it be too forward for me to ask for your phone number?"

He studied her face, like he might never see her again. Then he felt some relief when he saw her smile beginning to form again.

With a sly voice, and confident tone, she asked, "So, Mr. Shorty, how many times do you think some man has asked me for my phone number?"

At first he was a little stunned, and thought he should apologize, for overstepping boundaries. Then he realized she was just making a play on what he'd said earlier when she'd asked how tall he was.

She broadened her smile and began to look for something to write on.

While doing this, she said, "By the way, you are the third man today to ask for it. But to tell you the truth, I haven't given it out to anyone. Just promise me, Mr. Shorty, you better not turn out to be some kind of creep."

Then she laughed and threw her arms up, not finding anything to write on.

Shorty had never felt this pleased before. He started to dig in his pockets and pulled out the blue ticket from his wait for the cold shower. He thought that this had been his ticket to meet her in the first place.

Rosa asked a passerby for a pen and sat back down to write on the back of the ticket. She rubbed the ticket with her thumb and forefinger, and captured Shorty's eyes with her own. As she handed the ticket to the big American, a fresh, cool breeze flowed around them.

He put the precious phone number in his wallet and looked back over his sore shoulder to his boat. She playfully pushed him away to the final leg of his journey.

As he walked away, she called out, "Hey, keep yourself out of trouble. Bueno suerte."

When he reached the dock, he turned for one last look at her. Two young men had already approached her and appeared to be trying to create a conversation. Shorty breathed his relief when Rosa put her hands up and politely excused herself from the other men.

CHAPTER 16
THE BIG CROSSING

Each time the boat crested over a swell, it made a muffled thud as it slammed back down. Then it would ride the wave forward a few more feet.

The Cuban Weather Report had called for modest three-to-five foot seas throughout the night.

Shorty was crammed against the controls by the human mass behind him. The limp weight of living flesh seemed to roll from side to side. Three boats were loaded, as full with people as the deck could hold. The captains were given the option to wait until morning to leave. But the forecast was the best they could expect for the time of year. It was a unanimous choice to leave before dark.

The long wait was over.

Halfway into the Gulf Stream, the wind had picked up considerably. The boats were taking a pounding, but so far the two crawfish boats were running strong.

Every ten to twelve miles, there was an American Coast Guard cutter treading in the current. They were lit up like small cities and made the course easy to follow. It was a comfort to be on their radar in such a wild, black ocean.

An hour before, Pots and Shorty tried to reach the cement-hulled Family Boat by radio. It had taken a bearing too far to the west. But there was no answer, or reason for heading in a wrong direction.

Shorty had a real bad premonition when the running lights disappeared over the horizon. Two of the cutters left their spots at a high speed in that direction.

Later, they would find out that it would be one of the boats that never made it home.

It was a hard thing for both of the crawfishermen to imagine the fate of the smaller boat. But they had their hands full with sick Passengers and the aggressive sea.

Shorty felt a sharp pain on the back of his calf, so he looked down at his feet. Sitting beneath him on the deck was the elderly black woman with the white dreadlocks. She had plucked some hair from his leg to get his attention. Now she was beaming, a brilliant, four-toothed smile up to her new hero. He was absolutely taken with the wonderful smile. It made him laugh in a situation that had little room for anything funny.

He remembered another little stash that was kept in the hidden compartment, next to where he parked his gun. From under the dash, he pulled out a cork box that held an expensive bottle of Spanish brandy. It belonged to Dagger, and was hidden in reserve for a special occasion. Shorty figured that the old captain was already mad as hell, so he might as well take his bottle. He held the steering, wheel with his waist and used both hands to open the high-end liquor. He offered the first swig to his new girlfriend, Snowflake.

She was so flirtatious and funny that Shorty had to force himself to keep his eyes on the water ahead. Her face was glittering like phosphorous in the surf. She took a ridiculously long pull on the caramel-tasting brandy. Then she smacked her puffy, cracked lips and exhaled a loud, "Aaaaaaah!"

Shorty only took one hit from the bottle in order to keep his wits about him. But he enjoyed the few minutes of pure fun. He told her to keep the bottle and now she was really in love with him.

He turned all of his focus on climbing the next wave and the one hundred and eight responsibilities behind him.

Now almost every, wave was breaking over the bow. The boat was wet and the refugees dripped with the irritating salt water.

Behind him on the engine box was the mother and her infant. Her three daughters were huddled around as she nursed. The father of the beautiful family stood over them and intercepted every splash that would soak them. This image etched itself in Shorty's mind and would remain clear for the rest of his life. He knew that this family would become proud Americans.

Shorty had to spend much of his time hanging out of the side window, trying to see what was ahead of the struggling boat. His eyes burned and his vision was blurry. But he could see clumps of Sargasso seaweed floating by.

In some places, the wind and the tide will roll everything that floats into a scattered line. More often than not, they will harbor trash and debris that lurk just below the surface. Even in the daylight, it would be hard to see a floating log or big wooden spool that would have been discarded by one of the freighters.

By radio, he talked with Pots and they decided to change course a few degrees to try and get out of the weed line. The slightly different course made the vessels head more directly into the waves. Now it wasn't as much of an arm wrestling match to steer. It gave his bad shoulder a little bit of a rest.

After a few minutes, he felt a fluttering in the wheel. It ran up his good arm, and into the alarm part of his brain. Shorty was in tune with everything about the boat, and this did not feel good at all. It gave him a flush of anxiety to think that a mechanical problem could hit him so close to the end of this journey.

His instincts told his hand to take the control arm and throw it out of gear. But to stop the boat from making way in such a rough sea could cause it to be swamped. Instead he throttled down to a slower speed, and reached for the radio to call Pots. He hoped that the disabling debris would slide along the keel and avoid the propeller.

Just as he keyed the mike, the steering wheel started to rattle so hard that it threw his hands off. The boat quaked and a loud thumping sound came from under the rear of the boat. Eduardo was close by and quickly made his way through the crowd with a horrified face.

The refugees were now aware of the problem and were looking around at each other and forward to their captain. They were scared and looking for reassurance. A panic would only doom the effort to fix the problem.

Pots had already slowed down to match Shorty's pace, anticipating a possible need to set up for a tow. He sent his two mates to his stern with a heavy rope that was braided into a bridle, which was made for towing other boats..

Shorty breathed hard and spoke into the radio. "Shit! I friggin' ran over something and got it spun around the prop. Sounds like it wants to break the shaft."

He started into a long string of cuss words, but stopped when he saw the worry come over his people.

It was a severe moment. The boat was losing the power it needed to make way against the seas. A dangerous place to be with a boatload of people. Both men had to think and act quickly.

Pots said, "Relax, man. Keep it in gear and try to stay into the waves."

Then he jogged in front of the limping boat and eased back to a throwing distance.

Shorty handed the wheel to Eduardo and squeezed through the people. He stepped onto the gunwale and held the rail as he pulled himself up to the bow. The boat was lunging too much for him to stand, so went to his knees, and used them to grip the Samson post.

He could clearly see that everybody on the deck of Yogie's boat was watching him. The bigger boat was also packed with refugees.

All of the people on his own boat were straining their eyes to have a glimpse of the big American. They all had the intense look of worry for what he was doing. He was in the perfect place to be thrown from the boat.

The mate who worked for Pots had coiled the long rope and tossed it three times before Shorty was able to reach out over the water and snatch it. He muscled his boat closer, until there was enough slack to tie opposing half hitches on the post. Then he let the excess out until it was tight, and they were in tow. With each lunge over a wave, he could hear the fiberglass crackling from the stress.

Pots offered repeatedly to tow them the rest of the way in. But Shorty remembered a story of someone who pulled too much weight and it ripped the whole stern off of the boat. Then it sank.

They still had about thirty miles to go, and the ocean wasn't getting any friendlier. He couldn't shake the feeling that this wasn't going to work for too much longer. It could easily become a risk for both boats.

There was only one right answer for this situation. He would have to go under the boat and cut or saw away whatever was wrapped and tangled around the propeller. The safest way to make it home was on a boat that could make its own way.

The first time Shorty had to step off of a boat and into the belly of the ocean, it took a lot of internal encouragement. Who knows what could be hungry and swimming nearby. But after a few times, it became easier, just another part of the job. It was never something that anyone would really want to do. But it had to be done.

Running over discarded ropes and nets did happened. Sometimes the mates would even argue for the perilous duty. It showed their bravado, and disguised their fear.

But this time, they weren't close to shore, or in shallow water, during the daylight. Tonight he would have to cling tight under a boat that would be moving and the stern would be pounding with every wave. He would have to be able to hold his breath and be agile for the repeated diving to the rudder and propeller. His timing would have to be perfect, or the boat would come down on his back and crush him.

The convicts who stood along the stern respectfully parted for Shorty. He held the spotlight to show the crystal light blue water behind the boat. A massive wad of green cord shrimp net trailed behind the slow-moving vessel. It was tattered and spun up by the propeller below.

He had prepared a looped and knotted rope to hang onto once he was in the water. He tied off to the brace of the canopy and let it trail behind.

Eduardo nervously stood by to hand him the tools he would need.

Shorty jumped off to the side of the tangled mess and grabbed hold of it, to be pulled along with the boat. He reached up for an old dive mask. Then he spit on the inside of the lens and pushed it against his face.

His first work was done with his sharpened Cowhide knife. He cut away the big, visible pieces that dragged behind. They safely faded into the dark water behind them.

Before he went under the boat to attack the main mess, he took a breather. He held the looped rope under his arm and had a hand in the scupper hole that went through the stern at the deck. Each time the boat surged up and over a wave, he would count until it slammed down again. He would only get seconds to pull himself to the rudder and use a hack saw on the compressed wad of net. And seconds more to swim back out from under the hard, heavy hull.

Shorty looked up into the spotlight that was held by a serious-faced Eduardo. He covered his eyes until the stars and spots cleared. Then he saw many of the refugees straining to look over the stern and see him.

He looked down into the water and powered his way under the boat. This was the most scared he had ever been. It was the most dangerous thing he had ever tried to do.

With everyone's attention on Shorty, nobody noticed that Flaco had slowly worked his way to the front of the boat and was standing next to the controls. He crossed his arms and looked to the back, like he was also interested in the dramatic repair work that Shorty was doing in the water. He chose his moment and quickly turned the key and started the motor back up. Then he pushed the lever down that engaged the propeller in gear.

The big motor opened its throat and roared to life with Shorty holding his breath and working under the boat between the rudder, and propeller.

As he held back on his seedy smile and began to sneak back into the crowd, a chunky brown hand with purple fingernail polish quickly turned the key off and pulled it out.

A confused Flaco looked down at the dash as his forehead reverberated with a loud, sharp thud.

An empty liquor bottle won't break easy when it is used on someone's head. So Snowflake let him have it again.

The father of the beautiful family was the first to jump on Flaco. He took him to the deck and overpowered the killer in seconds. Snow flake took great delight in binding Flaco's arms and legs with duct tape. Then she wrapped some around his head and closed off his hissing mouth. The problem on the boat was now detained for the law enforcement in Key West.

When Eduardo heard the engine crank up, he turned the spotlight away from the water and strained to see back over everyone's heads.

Under the boat, Shorty had almost everything cleared. He was bearing down on the hacksaw, working on the last twisted knot.

The spotlight disappeared behind him at the same time the motor rumbled. Just as the tines of the big brass propeller began to turn, he kicked out to the underside of the hull. He came up in the darkness behind the boat and couldn't find the looped rope to hang on to.

After the motor shut down again, Eduardo threw the beam of light back onto the water behind the boat.

Following the fingers of some of the refugees, he found Shorty swimming ferociously to catch up with the tailing loop as the boat continued to be towed forward.

He was losing distance and would soon be lost from sight in the rolling waves.

Pots was where he needed to be in his own fly bridge. When he crested the next wave, it gave him the elevation to see as far back as the stern of Shorty's boat. He saw and heard the commotion and sensed there was a problem.

He couldn't slow down more than a few RPMs, or he would risk losing the momentum of gaining against the sea. But he tapped the throttle down and held the wheel strong.

Now everything for Shorty was in slow motion. He didn't hear the people screaming for him. The pain in his shoulder was gone, along with the rest of his feelings.

What was left of his ability to think made his long arms thrash towards the distant spotlight. The black water beneath him was thousands of feet deep. Now he was only an animal, in a wild fight to survive against the last great wilderness.

Parts of his body were beginning to contort from cramping just as he felt a rope land across his back. He flopped over on his side, and his hand, like a vice, gripped the thick stern line.

Eduardo had found the longer rope, coiled up under the tie off cleats, near the stern. With one try, he made the lucky toss. Everyone who was close, tried to help pull him to the back of the boat, including the convicts, who seemed as desperate as everyone else to see the big American survive.

Shorty stared up into the spotlight, confused and numb. Many pairs of hands reached down, and pulled him from his death.

That night the hungry ocean was jilted.

CHAPTER 17
VIVA LIBRE

A flood of people noise woke Shorty from his grayed-out state of consciousness. His reflexes snapped him into sitting up. He grew sharp very quickly, and felt the roll of the boat as it steamed ahead.

In a polite, raspy voice, he refused any help to stand. His knees were shaking, so he held onto the brace of the canopy until he felt steady.

Eduardo was behind the wheel; he smiled broadly when he saw Shorty back on his feet.

Shorty experienced a shower of relief when he realized that they were no longer in tow. As he made his way to the front, he felt the gentle touches from the refugees. Their adoring eyes followed his every move.

He gave Eduardo a strong handshake and hesitated to let go.

"Man, I got to thank you. If you want to keep the wheel for a while, I'm going up in the fly bridge and make sure we don't run over anymore shit."

His friend was exuberant to be considered a part of the crew.

Before Shorty swung up to the top, he told Eduardo, "When I stomp the roof above you, that means that I'll be taking over the wheel from up there. Meanwhile, I'll keep a good watch."

The night breeze parted and passed around his face and shoulders as he sat on his bench. He took the cool, sweet air into his lungs and felt the life returning to his body. Below him he left the smells of nervous sweat and vomit.

Now he could see the halo of light over Key West. A pink sky to his right fulfilled his hopes to see another sunrise.

Less than a day ago, this very moment was only a part of one of his daydreams. He was almost home, but instead of filling him with a grand feeling, worries of his captain's anger and his teetering relationship with Kim Sue became loud and alive in his mind.

Then his memory found the face of Rosa.

When he went to pull out his wallet, to have a look at the faded blue ticket, with her phone number, his stomach went hollow with a painful thud. He realized that he had forgotten to take it out of his pocket before he went into the water. Carefully he opened the soggy leather. He pulled out a wad of wet receipts and peeled off what was left of the precious handwriting.

He straightened it out and held it against one of the running lights. He focused and strained to see what she carefully wrote and trusted him with. But most of the numbers could not be read. Only her name, Rosa, stood out in perfectly-written calligraphy. He jumped into a panicky realization that he had been so mesmerized that he had forgotten to ask her last name. He racked his mind to try and come up with a way to reconnect with her. But he believed it was hopeless.

Feeling sorry for himself, he rolled up the gummed-up old ticket. With a long hesitation, he tossed it into the early-morning ocean.

He had thought that meeting the beautiful Latina was some sort of destiny. One that would become a different, and far better, direction in his life. Now that he had no way of finding her again, the possibility of a future with her had become his most powerful regret.

Between the battle under the boat and the loss of the precious phone number, Shorty had a rare moment of open emotion. He was alone and unseen by the people on his boat, so there was no reason to bury or hide his feelings.

It made him feel weak so he got down and went under the cap of the fly bridge. It was a small dry spot under the upper wheel box.

Now he felt completely alone and hidden, in a deep, safe cave.

Shorty lay on his side and pulled into a fetal position. When he closed his eyes, he wondered if this is what it's like to be dead. He felt the warm, salty water flow from the corners of his eyes and land on his arm. But after only a moment, a crack in his shell opened just enough to let one tiny sound reach into his sleeping mind—a wispy flight of feathers, backed up on the air, to land.

Shorty's eyes cleared enough to make out the familiar image, of one of those strange little canaries. It landed on the seat just inches from his face, bobbing its head and dancing on its twiggy legs. She began her chip chipping chatter, as she hopped up and down the length of the bench. Her beak and eyes kept darting back to the scrunched up fisherman who wasn't moving.

Shorty's eyes and mind were now filled with the actions of the Chip Chip. He began to feel his blood move in his veins. His pulse quickened and its throbbing showed on his wrists and neck. His shell fell off and his mind became clear and powerfully confident. In this sudden moment he felt like he had the power of a thousand men. No matter what else could go wrong, he had only one thought, and he said it out loud; "At least I'm free."

The Bird gave way and reached for the wind as Shorty climbed back onto his bench. He stomped the deck to signal that he was taking over the controls.

He had all of his clarity and his energy was buzzing. Each of his senses were hungry to once again feed on their own purpose. He was embraced by nature, and went forward on her power.

With pleasure he watched the Chip Chip, who stayed in the air around him until it sensed this boat was heading to the land. Then it fell back and became lost from sight.

 C380

For most of the crossing, every seventh wave broke across the boat and washed over the people below. But now the seas were beginning to lay down some as they approached the reef that grew upwards from the deep water.

It was in the gray light, just before dawn, when the Ocean comes alive. And Shorty was a part of it.

The dark blue water divided for the sharp bow as it cut through the phosphorescent sea. The bright green beads exploded and swirled into a glowing galaxy. As the boat passed through, it left a fiery tail in the wash.

Silver fish were spooked, and flashed randomly away from the churning bow. A school of Ballyhoo turned instantly together, and left the water for a few seconds.

Then a long slender Hound Fish skyrocketed from the deep and swam through the air beside him. Then it belly flopped onto the surface and dove from sight.

Shorty squinted to make out the large barnacles on the broad back of a Loggerhead Turtle. It seemed surprised to discover a boat plowing through the field of Man of Wars that it was grazing on.

The old skyline of Key West grew before him at the same rate that the sun rose to his right.

The growing happiness on the boat was beginning to filter its way up to the fly bridge. His throat fluttered with fresh excitement.

The two crawfish boats crossed the tricky reef, like those who had done so before. The shallow water loomed up under the hull. Shorty looked down at the white sandy holes for any signs of lobster. He easily dodged the coral heads that were covered with colorful aquarium fish.

When they were safely in the ship's channel, he climbed back down to the steering station in the cabin.

One hundred and eight sets of happy eyes beamed with admiration at the young man. He was taken back with the compliment of having so much attention.

Eduardo stood up from the captain's chair that he was reserving for Shorty. Then he puffed his chest out past his belly and started to sing an old Cuban folk song. A good number of the refugees joined in with "Viva Libre." They began to inject the lyrics with, "Viva El Capitan Chiquitico."

This was almost too corny for Shorty, who tried not to smile. He took over the wheel and acted like he needed to be serious and get back to his Job. Part of him was a little embarrassed. But the rest of him was beginning to embrace his pride. He was convinced that his mission was a good one. All of these people were now free.

The friendly water of Home was all around him. This damn trip was almost over with and he didn't care what came next.

He rounded the southernmost point and turned into the old Navy Docks. Everyone cheered but Shorty, who idled down and studied the American Debarkation Area.

A stout, African American Marine with a friendly smile stood on the concrete dock and guided them alongside a big brass cleat where they tied off. The mother of the beautiful family handed her infant to the big marine. Shorty noticed a single tear roll down his cheek as he gently held the blue eyed baby. When the mother followed she immediately went to her knees and kissed the ground of the free country.

This was the long-awaited destination of the Mariel Boatlift.

CHAPTER 18
THE BUBBA SYSTEM

An old cinder block wall, smooth and shiny from a dozen layers of yellow paint moved closer to Shorty's waking eyes. His reality came to in the form of a throbbing headache and sore ribs.

For the more rowdy members of the brotherhood, it was a familiar set of walls. They called it The Condo. An excellent place to cool down and sleep it off. The first coherent words were usually the same for everyone; they slapped their painful heads and said, "What the fuck did I do this time?"

For Shorty, this night in jail was a first. Until now, the gentle giant was known to be the one to keep a cool head. Now his nice guy image would be ruined forever.

During those years, in the lower Keys, there was a marvelous set of unwritten laws. But they only applied to the locals, or the few who were well connected. Doing things by the book was reserved for everyone else.

The Bubba System always worked something like this: Everyone's nickname was Bubba. As long as you didn't refer to someone's Mom as a Bubba, it was the appropriate way to greet another local. This worked out well for those who have a problem remembering names.

Shorty was like the son that Dagger never had. As it turned out, the old captain grew up with both judges in town.

The Friday night poker game was held at his house and usually included the Mayor, or at least one of the City Council Members, as regulars.

Shorty also had a sister who lived in town, and she was married to a lieutenant of the police force.

These were big advantages to have in such a small town—especially in a place that had a long history of floating just above, or maybe just beneath, the law. As long as no banks were robbed and nobody was killed, the key would open the heavy metal door and allow guests to walk the next morning.

Shorty limped onto the sidewalk and held his head with both hands. He hailed a taxi and sat in the back seat for the short ride out to Stock Island and the commercial fishing docks. Everything he saw was totally American, which still felt new.

Three weeks is a long time for a young, unstable couple to be away from each other. With all of the doubts, he had been having about Kim Sue, he still arrived thinking that everything would turn out to be fine. He was expecting to have a passionate reunion.

He was swollen with anticipation as he went to open the door of his apartment. His intention was to surprise her, and surprise her, he did.

Two horrified faces turned towards the doorway. They were in their underwear, on his couch, watching his TV, and drinking his beer. Not to mention that they were eating off of a plate of fried fish, which he had caught, and cleaned, and put in his freezer. The killing shot came when he noticed they were enjoying a bowl of his signature homemade tartar sauce.

The sailor quickly stood up to get dressed, while Kim Sue pulled a sheet over her head, thinking that would be a good place to hide.

At first Shorty did a good job with his composure. He threw his hands up, and backed down, saying, "Whooo! This can't be happening!"

He turned around and walked across the parking lot into a rundown watering hole named Stew's Bar.

He swiveled his bar stool around so he could watch his apartment. After firing down ten or eleven boilermakers, the shots and beers had made his body vibrate and his mind go dark.

Through the hole he kicked into his front door, he could see the Navy guy running for the bedroom, to escape out of the back window.

Shorty never saw the two burly sheriffs running at him from either end of the sidewalk.

They did a prison takedown on the young man. In a full run, one of the police hit him at the knees and the other hooked him by the neck. Shorty thunked his skull on the sidewalk—good thing he had a hard head. But he continued to fight back until he saw the shiny badge clutched in his big hand.

Shorty's attempt at violence was a flop.

The charges were for aggravated assault and resisting arrest. But they never showed up on any court docket.

Shorty stepped out of the taxi, thinking, *Thank goodness for the Bubba System.*

After a long telephone conversation that ended with a polite breakup, Shorty never returned to the apartment again.

A friend went over and gathered up his clothes in a garbage bag. Other than his guitar and a handful of notebooks, he gave the rest to Kim Sue, including the car, which was almost paid off. All of the possessions they shared together seemed tainted from the way it ended. The money that he almost died to make was probably being spent on the sailor.

Shorty believed making a clean break would be the best way to go. But he also had enough heart, to leave her able to survive.

Besides, at this point he was used to sleeping on the boat.

No distractions, no drama. He traded his comfort zone, for a little elbow room. With only nine weeks left before the season, more than 700 traps would have to be refurbished. Another 300 new ones would have to be built. He would have to turn his persona into a working fool. It was the best way that he knew to dig himself out of a mess.

He slowly walked through the maze of traps that were stacked six high behind the boat. The condition was bad but no different than in previous years. Breaking a few slats off, he crumbled the worm-tunneled wood and tossed it into a burn barrel.

As he approached the boat, he couldn't take his eyes off a big red tag plastered on the window. He read the notice: the government had moved to impound the boat.

The vessel was restricted from being moved or inhabited. Only essential maintenance and upkeep until the courts made a decision on the boats that had brought back refugees.

Shorty thought he had reached his bottom when he woke up in jail. But his bottom just kept getting deeper. Now he had nowhere to live. Not to mention that the boat was his only means of catching a few grouper and snapper for a little paycheck.

When the enormity of the work ahead filled his eyes, his heart took another deep plunge.

Shorty sat in the sawdust on his work table at the dock. No roof, no bed, no girl for bed, no food, except for a few cans on the boat. Noooo friggin' money!

"Looks like I'll be eating grits and grunts until the lobster decide to crawl," he said, glancing around to make sure no one was around to hear him talking to himself.

As he made fun of himself, he kept looking at the old trailer beside his traps. It had a rusted axle, with tires that had gone flat decades ago. Originally, it may have been a blue color, but years of fading in the hot sun rendered it into a colorless piece of junk. A few of the windows were cracked, but the inside was always dry. It served as a lockable storage shed for the more valuable gear that might decide to grow legs and disappear around a place like the docks. It was currently filled with rows of plastic bait cups and new boxes of trap rope. But every time in the past that Shorty had gone in there to get something, a big black scorpion or a giant wolf spider would jump from whatever he had in his hand. The place was infested, and it gave him the creeps.

But at least Dagger had forgiven him and let him keep his job, and this gave him a place to stay. At this point, the boat was looking awfully comfortable, but not accessible to poor Shorty.

After four insect bombs, he used a rake to empty everything out on the ground. He stopped long enough to watch one of the dying scorpions. It made him cringe to see something so mad that it was stinging itself on its own back. But it was still interesting to watch.

Then Shorty took a broom to the small space. With the gift of an old couch and the gas stove from the boat, he had a new home.

CHAPTER 19
THE CRAPPY TRAILER

The chucka-chucka sound of a nail gun blended with the nearby noise of labor. It echoed throughout the Basin, which was lined with battalions of lobster traps waiting anxiously to go to war.

A wobbly old air compressor flipped on with its loud, angry motor. It took a few long moments to build enough pressure to build another trap. It was a relief to the ears when it shut down again.

Shorty's American flag headband was soaked, heavy with sweat, and began to droop down over one eye. A stream of droplets cascaded, then splattered, on the white, waxy, cypress- wood slats.

As a man who stood all day in the hot sun and had to work at breathing the close air, Shorty found it was crucial for his mind to drift to a different place. If he thought about every little piece of work that passed through his hands, the evening would never come.

Shorty was always good for taking a little ride in his mind. He could conjure up a distant place and leave his tired body behind to do the work. Some cool and lazy paradise with Rosa, who was now the subject of almost every daydream. Even though it was the impossible daydream.

The ruination of the faded, wet ticket with her phone number had crushed all of his hopes. Not having a car prevented him from going to Jupiter and searching for her, and he cringed at his stupidity for not asking for her last name. He drew a frustrating blank when he tried to tried to remember the name of her family's company. Every quarter he could get his hands on was wasted in the pay phone asking for directory assistance.

He spent a lot of time reminding himself that she was way out of his league anyway. He foolishly thought that classy girls like her would never be attracted to a man who had nothing. Shorty figured that by now she had probably forgotten who he was. He had given up completely and marked it off as just some more rotten luck. But he could never forget the feeling he'd had when she was near.

Most of the boats that went to Cuba were still in some sort of legal limbo. Now, with only two weeks left before the opening of lobster season, nerves began to break among the fishermen.

Without the use of their boats, they would all become just a few more small businesses that went under. The whole industry was at stake. The forbidding-looking red tag glared at Shorty and it became like a red badge to discourage.

But many were hopeful that the same revolving politics that had seized their livelihood would change once again and set them all free. Some had made up their minds to put the gear out anyway—including Shorty, who believed he had no choice.

Perhaps a showdown with his own government, would be how he would start the season.

It was a normal part of the cycle for lobster men to endure the four months of the off season without pay. Those that toughed it out and finished the land work would hold their place on one of the producing boats on opening day, and hopefully the rest of the season.

Shorty's army of a thousand fresh, black traps would be lined up and ready to load on the boat. It had been a long summer of constant work and very little cash to survive with. The day to launch his troops couldn't come soon enough—if it ever came at all.

He sat down on a patch of slow-moving shade to rest and rehydrate. He flexed his knuckles and rubbed the cramps out of his wrists. The nail gun was heavy and hard to work towards the end of the day. But the pieces of new traps were adding up, stacked as high as the tall young man could reach. The walls of rebuilt traps made a maze around his crappy trailer and filled his work area.

As he chugged the melted ice water, he watched a young Marielito throwing a cast net.

Every throw he made between the boats opened up into a perfect circle. When he pulled it in, it spilled out hundreds of shimmering pilchards and glass minnows. The perfect bait for fishing on the reef.

No matter how many lessons Shorty took from the Kid, he could never get the hang of how to throw the tricky net. Even if he managed to open up the lead line, it would take the shape of a banana. Then it would crash on the water and, usually, scare the fish away. More often than not, it would get snagged on a piece of junk on the bottom, requiring Shorty to get into the oily water and work it loose.

The boy's name was Mario, but Shorty called his new helper the Kid. He was a cheerful teenager, and willing to work for free. Dagger hadn't come out to the docks for weeks, and Shorty needed the help.

The Kid and his father had come over from Cuba; they had a small boat tied off on the end of the crawfish docks. They quickly gained a reputation for producing a good catch of bottom fish.

One day, Shorty watched them unload nine hundred pounds of grouper, for just a day trip. What really impressed him was that they had no fish traps or bottom reels, which are normally used for harvesting the strong, heavy fish. He only saw two Hawaiian slings on their deck. He thought it was cool that these guys would free dive to ninety feet and could spear so many big money fish.

Whenever young Mario wasn't out on the boat with his father, he came around Shorty's space and pitched in with the work. For his young age, he could do anything that involved fishing, and he never asked for a dime. They fell into being a natural team and Shorty would make sure he had a place on the boat for the Kid when the Lobster were ready to be caught. The Kid also brought a little humor back into his otherwise bland and boring life.

Early on, they decided to speak each other's language in their conversations. This would force them both to have a better command of the two important ways to communicate. Of course, they began teaching each other all of the cuss words and foul expressions. Then they moved on to less important things like food and money.

One time Shorty struggled with his Spanish as he tried to talk about the old American cars he had seen in Havana. The Kid went on in English saying something about baseball. When they realized they were talking about two totally different things they fell into a good round of laughter.

Young Mario approached his new American friend and positioned himself to make one last cast with the bait net. These days, he was seldom without a smile.

Shorty said, "Hey, wait a minute, Kid. Show me, one more time, how to throw that damn thing."

Young Mario turned so Shorty could see how he coiled the rope and stacked the net in his one hand. When he put one of the leads in between his teeth, he mumbled, "Don't forget to open your mouth when you throw it."

Then he flung another perfect circle and pulled it in. He spilled the small silvery fish and topped off the bucket. Both men ran around the dock, capturing the flopping bait.

Then Shorty said, "Give me that thing."

He did everything exactly how he was shown. But when he went to make his throw, he forgot to open his mouth. He made a lion's roar that startled the Kid and made him run away from the dock. , Shorty spit as he pulled in the discombobulated net. Then he felt around his upper pallet and discovered one of his front teeth had broken clean in half.

Most men would have continued to lash out in anger with the painful screwup. But Shorty stood quietly still for a few seconds, then started to laugh. It grew into a hysterical few moments.

Young Mario cautiously stepped back onto the dock. He wasn't quite sure what to make of his gigantic new boss. One, whose reactions were so unpredictable.

Lately, Shorty's life may have been dull but it was full of hard luck. It seemed like new every day gave him another chance at making a stupid mistake. The aggravation of untangling massive mounds of trap rope, or missing with the nail gun and stapling his finger to a piece of wood.

At this point, having put a hole in his smile was par for the course.

After his breakup with Kim Sue a few months before, he had slid into the life of a hermit. On the weekends, some of the guys would come by and try to convince him to go downtown and cut loose. But for now he was more comfortable hiding behind the working side of Key West. Perhaps this would change once he could pull down a couple of paychecks.

He had built a wall of finished traps around his crappy trailer. It made him feel a little more secure and seemed to give him some privacy.

In the evenings, he would sit on a lawn chair and quietly strum his guitar, maybe sing a few old classic songs. He was careful not to be heard above the sounds around the docks. He played at the same low volume that he felt inside.

Though he was secretive about his ability to play, he was actually quite good. Every week he would add a few more popular songs to his repertoire. Unable to read music, he could learn and memorize everything by ear.

Whenever he added a new song to his list, he would play them all, getting a little better each time. It was always in the back of his mind to have another trade to fall back on. Sometimes he would think about getting back out there and playing with another band.

Before he finished for the night, he would spend a few moments on one of his originals.

Writing songs seemed to put him in a different zone. It was almost like a good buzz, only drug free. Being creative seemed to be his own best medicine. It always seemed to smooth him into a restful, peaceful night. He welcomed the feel good that his music gave him, especially during his toughest times. It never failed to remind him of his own sense of worth.

Young Mario appeared to have seen a familiar car entering the Fish House. He looked to be anxious to go over to his father's boat, but he was waiting for the OK from his new boss.

Shorty was easy to call it quits for the day. In Spanish he told the Kid, "Manana, temprano. Mucho workie, workie!"

The Kid nodded. "Si. Tomorrow, early."

They both smiled and bumped fists and made high fives. Then young Mario turned and took off in a jubilant rush.

Out of the corner of Shorty's eye, he caught the taillights of a big luxury car with tinted windows as it passed by. He thought that it was unusual to see such a fine vehicle around a dump like the fish house. Most of the time a vehicle like this one either belonged to one of the drug smugglers, draped in gold chains, or undercover law enforcement, pretending to be the smugglers draped in gold chains. From experience, he thought something might be up.

It caused him to have second thoughts about the Kid and his seemingly nice family. After his dealings with Flaco, he did everything to avoid those types. He hoped he was wrong, because he really liked the Kid.

Shorty opened the ice cooler by the door of his crappy trailer and fished out a floating pack of hot dogs. With his pocket knife, he cut it open and smelled it just to make sure it wasn't rancid. They seemed to be alright, so he tossed them in some boiling water.

"Mmmm," he said, "a feast for the beast."

He strained what was left of the ice with his fingers and fixed a stiff rum and ginger ale. He thought that it might feel good on his sore gums. Tonight must have been a special occasion because he had a hand full of Key limes to squeeze into his drinks.

As the night moved in, he heard a few more cars pull over to the Kid's boat. He was relived to see that the Kid's family was just having a shindig. It was common around the docks to have little parties on the boats. The spicy smells of Cuban food would drift across the water. Loud but friendly conversations hung in the balmy night air.

Shorty knew he would be more than welcome to join the fun, but he didn't feel much like socializing. Besides, he was almost finished with writing a new song about that crazy, beautiful Latina. At least now he could make her appear to him in the lyrics of a song.

He played the same melody over several times and tweaked some of the chords. The soft music filtered thru the wall of traps and whispered nonsense to the Marina. Then he put it away for the night. He reclined on the scratchy old couch and went into an immediate pig snore.

CHAPTER 20
NEW BEGINNINGS

Rosa pulled the keys from her purse and walked back over to her new car. This evening she was dressed to kill and feeling rather festive.

She had needed to postpone her visit to Key West for weeks. Finally, she had secured the release of her father's boat from the government. She managed the necessary repairs and it was quickly sold.

Now she was in the midst of a feel-good reunion with her new brother and his loveable family. The little sisters called her Aunt Rosa and the parents were enamored with her for daring the dicey rescue of their son.

Young Mario had to get past his obvious crush and become a stand-in for the brother that she had been unable to bring back from Cuba. He knew he was too young for her but she would always be the angel who brought him back to life. And she never gave him any encouragement to think otherwise. She showered him with the love of a real sister and a friend.

She also had a few of her Key West friends join them for the little boat party. They shared plenty of the mother's good cooking, along with some beer and wine.

It was just first dark when her pretty silhouette pulled a six-pack of ginger ale and a few bags of chips from the trunk of her car. She was a little giddy, but not tipsy. The small get-together had returned a grand smile to her face.

As she closed her car up, a quiet little breeze of acoustic guitar music brushed against her cheek. She turned towards the darkness of the docks and tuned in to the faint, but nice, sound.

At first, she thought it might have been somebody's radio or cassette player. But she quickly knew that it was live music, hiding somewhere in the labyrinth of traps nearby.

She wasn't sure why but she stayed in the darkness, close to the boat, and listened for a few moments. Her dreamy eyes slowly closed, and she leaned back against her car. The light music with a man's voice entered into her mind and body and didn't seem to want to leave.

When the car keys slipped from her hand and hit the hard pan gravel at her feet, it startled her out of the strange spell that warmed her soul.

She quickly skipped back into the safe light of the boat party and pulled her red high heels off. She smiled and handed her things to Young Mario, who had a concerned look waiting for her. Before she stepped back onto the boat, she took one more long, curious look into the darkness behind her.

Like a protective brother, Young Mario gave Rosa his hand and helped her on board.

"Is everything OK?" he asked, looking fiercely at the darkness.

Much impressed with his improving English, she said, "Yes, yes, it's all good. It's all great."

Then she entered back onto the boat and into her friendships. She sat on the stern, and rocked easy to the highs and lows of laughter from the small party.

The song that she could barely hear in the darkness seemed to have found a home in her mind. It puzzled her, because she only heard it once. She couldn't quite discern the words, but the enchanting melody stayed with her.

This was a new experience for her, and it made her feel a little sparkle of euphoria. It seemed like a mysterious gift from an anonymous sender.

The breakup with her boyfriend back home had been long and difficult. It left her emotionally drained and a little short of her usual passion for life.

She had met an interesting young man in Cuba, but he never called, and made her feel like she had been jilted. She decided to take a break from dating anyone for a while.

⋘⋙

Just before lunch the next day, Shorty and the Kid finished dipping the last group of traps. The big square, metal tank was filled with a mixture of Bunker C Tar and diesel. The black stain helped to preserve the traps for the long months under the corrosive seawater. It was the sort of job that required wearing clothing meant to be thrown away.

Shorty soaked a rag with paint thinner and wiped his hands and arms up to his shoulders. Then he left the rag on a trap for the Kid to use. He walked up to the boat to use the sink and some dish soap to finish cleaning, the burning chemicals from his skin. When he washed his face, the stubble reminded him, that one of these days, he would have to shave. Then he was curious to see his broken tooth. He took a two-second glance at a hand held mirror, and was frightened by his own face. He was a mess.

He took out his pocket knife and cut a long strip from a clean towel, fashioning a raggedy headband. Then with a crooked smile, he slipped into his new white boots. He had to bum the money from Dagger to make the purchase and finally escape the stench of the old orange pair. Now that he felt clean, he started looking for some work to do that wasn't so filthy.

The fine new car pulled in front of the opening in the traps to the work area. When Rosa got out from behind the wheel, she walked over to give Young Mario a big hug. She was on her way back up north and wanted to stop and say goodbye to her new brother.

Young Mario's eyes lit up when he saw her, but he put his black hands out to show her not to get too close. In fairly good English he said, "I'll have to take a rain check on that hug."

Rosa looked up at the stacks of traps and the rest of the organized work area with the look of amazement. "Wow, so this is the new job you were been telling me about?"

"Mucho trabajo y no dinero."

Rosa frowned. "What! You did all of this work and haven't gotten paid?"

Then she remembered her cousin who was a lobster man and would also wait for the season to reap his rewards.

"No, I didn't do all of this, myself." Then he cupped his hands and called up to the boat. "Hey, Chiquedico, come over here and meet my angel."

The named passed through Rosa's mind and left the image of the Man she met in Cuba.

She cocked her head toward Young Mario and cautiously asked. "Did you say Chiquedico?"

"Yes, the gringo is my friend, and also my new Boss."

Rosa crossed her arms and put her forefinger to her bottom lip. "Is this gringo a tall gringo?"

Young Mario sensed her growing concern. "He seems to be a real nice guy. Besides, he is the only American that will talk to me."

She stiffened up, knowing that she was about to run into the big gringo who sweet talked her out of her telephone number and then blew her off.

From the other side of the traps, Shorty thought, "Angel, hmm? Sounds like the Kid has got himself a little girlfriend. I better go take a look."

On the way over, he opened up his always ready imagination, searching for something really ridiculous to say, perhaps to embarrass the Kid in a teasing sort of way. Or maybe just something to make a funny first impression.

When he turned the corner with a smile, he stopped like he hit an invisible wall. Everything in his sight blurred into a hazy frame that surrounded the crystal, clear, sight of Rosa. He thought he just walked into the middle of a miracle.

After losing all of his hope and giving up on her completely, there she was.

Rosa didn't look very happy and Shorty was puzzled by her hostile demeanor. They faced each other without a word.

The ever-present smile of Young Mario dropped into a concerned seriousness. "Hey! Do you guys know each other?

Shorty looked at the Kid and raised his brows even higher than his wide open eyes. Then he exhaled a resigned breath and continued his silence.

Rosa sweetened her voice for her new brother and said, "Yes. Would you mind if I have a few moments alone with your friend?"

With her arms still crossed and her foot tapping with aggressive energy, Rosa entered into a stare-down with the very confused Shorty. She almost said something, but quickly stopped her mouth from moving. Her eyes broke through his and continued on to the bottom of his soul. She was waiting for him to open his mouth, so that she could give him a good verbal slap.

Shorty was honestly perplexed. He couldn't for the life of him figure out why she could be so upset. He believed that running into her again had some sort of mystical reasoning behind it. He felt extremely relieved and filled with joy to be blessed with this powerful coincidence. He wanted to believe that his sentence to hard luck had been served and he was ready to be released into the arms of one who took the center of all of his dreams.

He had to say something to break through this glacial ice.

Shorty opened his arms and stepped slowly forward. "Rosa, what's wrong? My goodness, what have I done? I am really so happy to run into you again."

Rosa snapped back at him; "It's not what you did, it's what you didn't do!" She threw her hand out, and said, "Who do you think you are to play games with my feelings?" She put her hands on her hips and proclaimed to the wounded-looking Shorty, "I never give out my phone number to anyone." Her voice choked a little, like she wished that she was wrong for scolding him. But she continued on. "You must have a Little Black Book that you show off to all of your men friends. What? Do you just go around and collect your opportunities with unsuspecting women to feed your big, fat male ego?"

Now that Shorty was beginning to understand where she was coming from, he had to interrupt her. His own insecurity had convinced him to believe that she didn't care if he called her, or not. He smiled and said softly, "Rosa, it got wet."

She stopped her Assault and looked up to him, not understanding what he just said.

"What?"

"Yeah, you're phone number got wet when I had to take a swim under the boat to get the propeller untangled during the crossing. I couldn't read the numbers, or believe me, I would have called. I would have called you a hundred times by now."

He looked at her confused but almost relieved-looking face. Then he finished approaching her and went for her hand. His eyes had now reached into her soul and she could see the honesty.

She still wasn't sure of how she could be so completely wrong, so she pulled her hand back. She felt like running back to her car and trying to think this one out.

Feeling the rejection, Shorty slowly turned and started walking toward his crappy trailer.

She watched him walk away and a push from no one behind her forced her to follow. She had to run a little to catch up with his long strides. She slipped her hand up under his elbow and slowed him down to once again see his eyes.

She said, "I'm sorry. How could I have known? I really am sorry for scolding you. I hope you don't think I'm a bitch."

Shorty looked down at her watery eyes and a smile that wanted to grow. It didn't take much to recapture his heart.

They were standing next to his lawn chair in front of his homeless man's home. Once again, after the long months apart, they were close to each other and feeling good about it.

When the young man opened up his smile, Rosa put her hand to her mouth to cover her surprise. "Shorty! What happened to your tooth?"

At this point, any humiliation he might find from his rough condition could only be laughed about. He pulled his lip up to show her the new hole in his mouth.

"What happened?"

In a matter of fact way, he said, "Ah, I got into a fight with a cast net. As you can see, the cast net won and beat the hell out of me."

She quickly understood. "Oh, so you forgot to open your mouth when you let loose? It's funny, but one of my uncles lost all of his teeth in the front by making the same mistake. Those crazy throw nets." Then she added, casually, "Someday I'll show you how to use one correctly."

If I could get her to teach me instead of the Kid, Shorty thought, *I could pretend to never learn and keep her coming back every day for the next ten years. Hell it might just take that long anyway.*

Rosa took a good look around the work area and with a compassionate voice asked, "So is this where you live?"

Before he could answer, she saw the guitar propped up against the couch inside the trailer. Her face shot back to him as she realized that he must have been the one she'd heard playing the night before. But for now, she kept her knowledge of it quiet. The mystery of his music had made her look in his direction. And now, by complete coincidence here they were, together again. This was becoming a very interesting accident.

Rosa was mostly rational, but like many of her people, she was also a bit superstitious. She trusted in some of the unexplainable chances that come along in life. Her heart was now opening again and it told her to follow this one.

Shorty opened his hands and said, "Yes, Rosa, this is my lovely little world. That's my crappy trailer, complete with all of these luxury surroundings." He looked at her and offered a silly smile. "Hey, at least it's waterfront property."

She clung to his arm as they walked up to the boat and the anxiously waiting Young Mario.

He was glad to see that his two friends were acting like friends. Though he was almost a little tiffed that she was holding so tightly to Shorty's arm.

As they stepped onto the dock, Rosa rushed over to Young Mario, who was now cleaned up and waiting for his hug. He blushed, but loved every bit of the attention.

She turned to Shorty and asked. "So what do you think of my new brother?"

Shorty said; "New Brother? How does that work? What do you do? Go out and rent some guy for a while and call him a brother?"

Shorty's confidence seemed to be holding up as long as he could get away with his corny humor.

Then he asked; "So how do you know the Kid?"

Rosa paused for a moment and sat on the gunwale of the crawfish boat. "I guess you can say that I smuggled him out of Cuba. He was an escapee from the military and we hid him on our boat for weeks." As Shorty sat next to her, she looked sad. "I never did find my real brother, Catanno."

Shorty turned to her, and remembered the weight of Esperanza's disappointment, so he could feel her sorrow. But when her story sank in, he realized how courageous this little lady must be. What she had done for Young Mario was the greatest risk to be taken against the Cuban government. He learned a healthy respect for her personal power.

Then he told her about the swimmer he saw on the first day.

"Oh, yes," Rosa said. "I heard about him. Did you know what they did to that one?"

When she explained about the televised execution, they both showed pain for the conditions in Cuba.

He looked over to the Kid and tried to imagine him wearing a uniform. Shorty would look at him differently now that he understood what he must have gone through.

Young Mario heard the crumbling rocks under the tires of a beat-up old fish truck. He looked to the entrance of the fish house and saw the unmistakable outline of Dagger in his old truck.. It was impossible to not recognize the clunker and it's driver. The two front fenders were crunched and rusted from ancient, unreported wrecks. The rear bumper was dragging from the bait wire fix. It clanged as the slow moving pickup crawled over the pot holes.

Shorty felt a flush and sounded a relief. "It's about time the old man showed up, now that the work is almost done."

He got up and told Rosa, "That's the captain. He's most likely coming out here to raise some hell. Watch, he'll probably pull down one of my traps and act like he needs to fix my work."

She looked over that way with a bright interest, and not a hint of intimidation.

As the old man pulled up behind Rosa's car, Young Mario stepped up and saluted the air to announce. "El Capitan de Langosta."

Rosa smiled at Mario's greeting for the lobster boat captain.

Shorty asked the Kid to go lend a hand with the last-minute materials Dagger was supposed to bring so they could finish the work. He turned to see that Rosa was still sitting and looked like she was feeling sobered from the conversation about Cuba. He gently put his fingers under her chin. She looked up to him, as he said, "Hey, just think of how many people you have gifted with freedom."

A quick smile came back to her face as she took his hand and stood to meet the legendary captain.

Dagger inspected the army of traps while he continued to approach his boat.

Shorty noticed that he was carrying a grocery bag and a bottle of Spanish Brandy. This is how he usually looked when he intended on taking a boat ride. It seemed like a strange thing, considering they still couldn't use the boat.

Young Mario was carrying two fifty-pound boxes of nails and had a comically, strained look on his face. He plopped them down on the dock and breathed back into a cheerful, smile.

Before the Old Captain stepped over on to his boat, Shorty relieved him of the bags. Dagger never even acknowledged his first mate. His silly eyes were locked onto the beautiful young lady who was standing next to his boat.

Shorty shook his head, and laughed at the blatant flirtation as he went up into the cabin to stow the food.

The old captain held a big grin and walked directly over to Rosa and introduced himself in the old school way. He bowed at the waist and then kissed her hand without giving up any of his engaging eye contact. She was beaming and very flattered as she went along with the elaborate introduction.

Then Dagger gave her a broad smile and boldly said, "What can I say? I'm Latin." Then he rolled his eyes in a kooky way.

She really laughed hard and felt instant friendship with this older man.

Dagger was usually cranky by this time of day.

If it was after lunch, Shorty knew enough to open a bottle and have some clean ice on hand. It was a sure-fire way to bypass the residual grumpiness of a hangover.

He hadn't seen his captain for over a month and didn't really expect to see him any time soon. He had the feeling that the old man had something up his sleeve. He was just too cheerful and was also whistling some old country tune. This out-of-character behavior made Shorty a bit nervous and unsure about what to expect.

As Dagger walked up to his place at the wheel, he snarled, "Hey, man! You've been checking the motor? How about the bilge? No leaks?"

Shorty responded; "Everything is running good, except the batteries need to be run up."

The Old Captain waved the Kid over and spoke to him in Spanish. It felt like he was leaving Shorty out of the fold. Then he cranked up the motor.

Young Mario found a scraper and jumped up on the gunwale and started to remove the mean-looking red tag.

Then Dagger turned to Rosa and cordially asked her if she would like to go fishing for a few hours.

Shorty's pulse was racing from what appeared to be the long-anticipated release of the boat. A flood of relief washed over him and left him standing under his own power once again. Now he knew that he could be among the first to drop traps on the good spots during opening day.

The old captain continued to ignore Shorty and went to the stern to cast off the line. Then he stopped, slapped his forehead and said, "Oh, shit! I almost forgot." He turned back to the cabin and pulled a roll of paper work from the brown bag that had the bottle of Spanish brandy. He motioned for Shorty as he went over the official looking papers. Then he took one out and jabbed the young man in the chest with it.

When Shorty read the release form, he smiled. "How in the hell did you pull this one off?"

Dagger just beamed. "Hey, the Bubba System works every time."

Then he handed the young man a folder and told him to read it.

Rosa stood beside him as he opened it. On the first page he could see his name written as the documented captain of this boat.

Dagger smiled big and poked at the folder. "This means that I am officially retired. And that means you can't bug me about coming to work anymore." Then he gave the enraptured young man a very firm handshake. "She's your baby now."

From the side, Rosa threw her arms around him, then she let loose and cheered for him. Young Mario joined in with the applause.

A cool, refreshing breeze flowed into Shorty's lungs. After so many weeks of having such sour luck, he had never expected a day like this. He looked at Rosa and then back at the folder. He wondered how everything he truly wanted could fall into his lap in just a few minutes. His power and his purpose were doubled as he gratefully entered into these wonderful new beginnings.

Dagger cut through the air with his hand and said, "Finito!" [I'm finished] and symbolically resigned the wheel to Shorty.

Then, just like he was placing an order at a fish market, he said, "I got some family coming down over the weekend and I want at least three groupers, preferably scamps. Then I need about twenty yellow tails, around a pound a piece."

Then he picked up an old wood box with the hand line gear and walked to the stern. He said to Young Mario, "Hey, boy, let me see that fresh-looking bait you caught."

Shorty knew exactly where to go and snag some good eating-sized, fish. Over the years he noticed that most of the boats didn't start fishing until they reached the reef. They always passed over the shallow, sandy bottom out front. He knew the occasional rocky patches that were close inside attracted plenty of sea life. They were mostly undiscovered and easy to make a good catch in a short period of time.

As they idled out into the channel, Rosa stood on the starboard side. The wind pushed the hair back from her face. She was noticing every little scene along the way.

The wet tide line on the sea wall was encrusted with razor oysters and barnacles. Just under the clear water, they opened up with fan-like features that filter their meals. A great blue heron back flapped into a weightless landing on the Point. She smiled at the silvery schools of bait fish that evaded the passing boat. They darted away, confused, but swimming as one.

Though Rosa seemed preoccupied with the astounding array of wild life, she could feel Shorty's eyes whenever he looked her way. She quietly hoped that she looked good to him.

Then she heard his friendly voice. "Hey, Rosa, come over and check out the manatees." He was looking in the water on his side. "It looks like two, maybe three. Dang, I've never seen these things before."

He was always excited to see something new in the ocean.

She skipped over to him, and said, "Oh, cool! We see lots of these guys up where I live."

Together they observed the slow, lumbering giants of the waterways. The meandering sea cows are purely peaceful but they are vulnerable to fast-moving boats. Shorty pointed out the propeller scars on the grassy back of the biggest one. He stepped back to the wheel and idled down a bit more to avoid doing any damage to the thousand-pound animals.

When the boat came out of the channel and forged into the swells, Shorty pushed the throttle down to half way. Then he leaned over to check his gauges. He set a course for the inshore Patches, with the excited anticipation of hunting down some fish.

The water went from lime green to clear as the mottled rocky bottom rose up to make it shallow. Then he slowed down into a circle and took it out of gear.

Young Mario had already tossed a few strategic handfuls of chum to excite the water around them. The chopped bait fish fanned out and glittered its way to the bottom. They could already see the flashes of the aroused yellow tail around the boat.

Dagger assumed that the girl would need a lesson on how to work the Cuban hand line and began to show her how. Rosa just listened with a smile and humored him. Then she took over the monofilament line like an old pro. Within seconds, she had the first fish on and skillfully made it swim to the boat.

Shorty left the wheel and watched the bottom while the other three had fun. When he saw more sand than rock, he urged everyone to pull in the lines. Together they had eleven fish on the first pass. Then he moved the boat to a different spot to make another drift.

With every fish that was caught Rosa was the maker of excitement. Barefoot and out-fishing both men, the lady became like a little girl. She was exuberant and purely innocent. Without any effort, she appeared to be the centerpiece of everything natural.

As Shorty watched, a breezy thought cooled its way through his mind. This image might become his privilege for a long time to come. The thought was almost too comfortable to keep. But he couldn't help but have the feeling that he was no longer single. But still he was unsure that such a wonderful fate could be his.

A single soaring Pelican decided it couldn't wait any longer. The fish and the bait all over the deck of the boat was too much of a temptation. It made a long and graceful glide to land on the aft. But only one of its webbed feet found the gunwale. It struggled to regain its balance, but flopped backwards head first into the water. Everyone saw and laughed at the big, clumsy seabird's comical crash landing.

Rosa wrapped the line back on the spool and took a break from the biting fish.

As Shorty watched her approach, she went from a satisfied smile to a more serious look. *Uh oh*, he thought, *what's she gonna come up with, now?* He kind of liked the way she could be so totally unpredictable. The nervous boy woke up inside of him.

She found his moving eyes and held on to them. Then, in a matter of fact sort of way, she asked, "Hey, Shorty, do you have any crackers on board?"

"What?"

"Crackers. You know, those crunchy things we eat with soup."

He paused for a few seconds to figure out the request. Then he fished around in one of the cabinets and pulled out a can and shook it. "Sounds like there are a few left, but I can't guarantee how fresh they are. They could be years old. I wouldn't eat any of those things."

She put her finger to her lips. "Shh. Be quiet and don't make any quick moves."

Shorty scrunched down to her level and his eyes opened wide in a funny way. He rolled them to the left, and then to the right.

Without seeing any reason for what she was doing, he whispered, "Rosa, what the heck are you talking about?"

"Shush! Just watch, and you'll see."

She crumbled one of the soda crackers and carefully sprinkled the crumbs on the dash and around the sink.

It was then that Shorty saw one of those little Chip Chip birds, quietly perched on the radio just above his head. He liked to believe in his power of awareness and he wondered how the rare little bird had landed on the boat without him seeing it.

He quietly watched as Rosa cooed and coaxed it down onto the dash. One by one, the skittish little bird ate the crumbs, and came closer to her open hand. Within a few, patient, moments, it hopped onto her finger.

Shorty was dumbfounded. Never in his life had he ever seen a wild creature come so easily to any human. The experience gave him rushes all over, and also gave him the reason to believe that this lady was special, indeed.

Just as Dagger landed his third grouper, he bellowed with his dominant voice, "Hey, Cappy, take us back in."

The gruff noise of the old man startled the fragile little bird. It entered back into the welcoming air where it lived most of its life.

Rosa and Shorty both watched as it banked back and forth in the open cabin, just missing any walls or windows. Then she left the boat on the port side. The Chip Chip took an easy ride on the wake of wind made by the speeding boat. After a few minutes, it took a dive at the head of the old human who had interrupted its rest on the boat.

Dagger stood in the open on the stern and began cleaning the fresh, and soon-to-be delicious, fish.

Without seeing what just buzzed the back of his head, he brushed it away, like it was just an annoying insect.

Seconds after the fish parts hit the water, the first seagull arrived, excited by his ever-present hunger. He was quickly joined by many more, appearing out of every direction.

The space became too dangerous for the little land bird to stay. Besides, this friendly boat was heading to land. The wrong direction for her nature to follow. She fell back into the distance and made a turn to the open sea.

While the men were busy working the boat, Rosa kept her eyes on the Chip Chip until it faded into the haze that hung above the deep water.

She was feeling its adventure and thought deeply about its nonsensical course. She began to understand that she was witness to the greatest of courage in one of the smallest of creatures. Every living thing is born to search for survival. Only the bravest will fight it's way to a better life and provide more strength to the next generation.

Rosa was a deep thinker, not unlike Shorty. Always looking for the best answer to every question. She took a long, unobserved look at the young captain, who looked so proud behind the wheel of his new adventure. From behind, she gently clutched his arm.

This simple touch caused his eyes to close and he swam with the wave of assurance. Until now, he had been a virgin to the feelings of real love. The kind that he always knew existed, but believed he might never find. It made him feel complete to know that her golden brown eyes were there to smile for him.

With a warm, sultry look, she squeezed between the wheel and the captain's chair. She leaned back into him and rested her head just under his chin.

Shorty steered the boat with one hand and ventured the other on her hip.

Rosa pulled his arm around her waist, and they joined each other's comfort. Stroking his hand with her small, soft fingers, she quietly hummed a melody that was going through her head.

Shorty enjoyed the slight vibration against his chest. After a few moments the soft notes of her music began to sound almost familiar. It was suspiciously similar to the song he had been writing about her. He was too private about his songwriting for anyone to hear. So this made no sense to him at all. Then he could see her cheeks rising with her smile, as though she knew what he was thinking.

She softly spoke to him. "Last night I was on Mario's boat and when I went to my car I heard someone playing music. It sounded good to me. I hope you don't mind if I listened in, for a while."

Shorty kissed her hair and whispered. "Of course not." Then he flexed his arm and held her even closer.

From back at the stern, Dagger and the Kid began laughing and teasing the two love birds who were driving the boat. The old man began singing in a sorry, off-key voice. Besame, besame, mucho."

Shorty knew the song—Kiss me, kiss me more—and his face turned red. But Rosa looked back with a silly smile. She knew exactly how to shut them up.

She touched Shorty's cheek and they saw into each other's soul.

The whole world went silent when they kissed.

ABOUT RUSTY

Hi, everybody. I'm Rusty Jaquays and I am at that boomer age were retirement is smiling and waving at me from a closer distance every day. But I still have a great deal to accomplish before I can bask in the warm light of days with little worry.

While most of my contemporaries are fast becoming grandparents, I am the older father of young children. A few years back my beautiful wife handed me an infant girl. Mind you, I was a big strong man; but this powerful event brought me to my knees. Now we have another daughter and I know that I have found the treasure I was meant to find, our family.

So there's still a lot of pork chops and bread to bring home, but I feel privileged at my age to enjoy a few more hilarious school plays—even though I'm still racking my aging brain to understand teenage drama.

Before I finally settled into this good life, I was known to be a wild human. No one, including myself, would have ever believed that I could be tamed enough to become a peaceful family man.

By the time I left high school I was no stranger to change. The interstate system became my home as I hitchhiked my way into the future. I was hungry for food a few times, but I was always starving for a fresh new experience. I worked my way from one region to the next, discovering my strengths and humbled by my weaknesses.

By the mid-seventies my road ended at the southern-most point of the U.S., in Key West, Florida. The only way for me to go any farther would have been by boat. It was here in this always interesting town where I began my first real career. I found work on a lobster boat and chased the adventure of harvesting seafood. This dangerous but exhilarating profession provided me with too many stories to tell.

It's always been my best habit to take notes on most everything that has affected me. It's like magic to see a blank page become a story or even a song. Like good therapy, creative writing has saved some of my good times to be savored once again; but more important it's a way to purge the negatives from my mind and leave them harmless on paper. This makes more room for the positive, which is something I could never have enough of.

The story of **Chip Chip** *is based on my first-hand experience with the Cuban boat lift in 1980. This was a mass exodus of historic proportions that earned a controversial reputation. I turned that once-in-a-lifetime experience into my first novel.*

The main character, Shorty, is a young first mate on a Key West lobster boat chartered to go into the repressed ruins of this communist country and retrieve eleven political refugees. During his month of danger, Shorty finds courage that he never knew he had and some unexpected romance.

The title, by the way, is based on a true story about a legendary and rare wild canary commonly called Chip Chip, a tiny land bird that chooses to survive in the vast, dangerous ocean and reminds us about the power of freedom.

Made in the USA
Charleston, SC
15 May 2016